PURRFECT BACHELOR

THE MYSTERIES OF MAX 45

NIC SAINT

PURRFECT BACHELOR

The Mysteries of Max 45

Copyright © 2021 by Nic Saint

Edited by Chereese Graves

www.nicsaint.com

Give feedback on the book at: info@nicsaint.com

facebook.com/nicsaintauthor
@nicsaintauthor

First Edition

Printed in the U.S.A

PURRFECT BACHELOR

An eye for an eye

Thirteen years ago, five confirmed bachelors were accused of a hit-and-run accident that left Poppy Careen dead on a quiet residential street. Now Poppy's mother asks Odelia to finally get justice for her family. But when Odelia pays a visit to one of the five men, she finds he's been murdered. The most likely suspects are the Careens, especially Poppy's dad, who never fully recovered from the death of his little girl. But soon other suspects pop out of the woodwork, and when more bodies are discovered, it becomes clear that there's a lot more to this case than meets the eye.

CHAPTER 1

Dooley and I were hard at work doing what we do best—namely napping, after having eaten our fill in delicious kibble—when Odelia's phone rang. We were in her office, assisting her in the writing of one of her articles. Simply by being there, we provide our human with much-needed inspiration. In other words: we provide a vital service.

Or at least that's what we like to think.

"Yes?" she said in a distracted voice as she frowned at her attempt to write a fascinating account of the dog show that had recently taken place in town. Not sure why anyone would want to look at dozens of dogs and pick a so-called 'best in show.' I mean, it's dogs. Enough said. Now if it had been a cat show, that would be a different story. Unlike dogs, cats are actually nice to look at. We're graceful, clever, attractive… I could go on and on.

Odelia frowned, and glanced in my direction. I heaved a little sigh, for I knew exactly what that look signified: another case was looming large on the horizon.

You see, Odelia might be a mere small-town reporter, but lately she's been simply inundated with requests from people in need of her assistance. She took on one case, managed to bring it to a satisfying conclusion for all concerned, and soon word spread and now everyone who's facing some issue great or small comes a-knocking, hoping she'll do the same for them. It's very tiring, I must say. Then again, there is something imminently gratifying about helping a person or persons in need. Not least because there is usually a nice treat involved if we manage to do a good job.

"Looks like we've got another case, Dooley," I said, stirring my friend.

"I was dreaming" he announced, smacking his lips.

"Of kibble?"

"Of the baby."

"Oh."

It was a point we'd both spent a lot of mental energy on lately. Odelia recently announced that she's pregnant, and I honestly have to say I don't know whether we should be happy or sad. Babies are an unknown quantity, of course, not unlike a loose cannon. They might be a cause for concern, or a cause for great joy, depending which side of the cannon you're facing. In other words it's hard to know what to expect before they actually pop onto the scene. The problem is, unlike a cannon, loose or otherwise, you can't return a baby to sender. Once they arrive, they're... there, if you see what I mean. They're not going away, and will probably be something we have to deal with... forever!

"Let's go, you guys," said Odelia, grabbing her phone.

"Where are we going?" I asked.

"That was Mrs. Kristina Careen on the phone just now," she said. "And it seems that she needs our help."

"Don't they all," I murmured, but nevertheless got up from my favorite blanket.

When duty calls, and all that.

· · ·

On the drive over, Dooley was conspicuously quiet, then finally blurted out, "So when is the baby due, Odelia?"

"Oh, not for months," she said as she leisurely steered her aged pickup through early morning traffic.

"Months? Or years?"

She laughed. "I think that's a different species you're thinking of."

"Are there species where pregnancy takes years?" I asked, interested. It would be nice, of course, if it took Odelia nine years to deliver this baby instead of nine months. In nine years I might finally be ready to greet this bundle of joy into our lives. Or not.

"Dinosaurs, maybe?" Dooley suggested.

"That might explain why they went extinct," said Odelia, who seemed in a particularly good mood this morning. Must be all of those pregnancy hormones, I guess. Odelia's mom Marge and her grandma had been talking a lot about the glow Odelia had. Though to be absolutely honest I hadn't noticed any such phenomenon. Not even in the dark.

"So how many months?" asked Dooley. "Twelve? Twenty-four?"

"More like nine," said Odelia. "The usual, you know."

"Harriet said that pregnant women develop a lump," said Dooley. He sounded worried. "So do you have a lump already, Odelia? And if you do, does it ever go away again?"

"I think Harriet was probably referring to a bump, not a lump," said Odelia with the same placid calm she usually displays when answering Dooley's barrage of questions. I guess she figures it's good practice for when the kid is born. Kids are notorious for asking a lot of inane questions. "And yes, it does go away again. Or at least I hope it does."

Dooley swallowed away a lump of his own. "Where is this bump going to be? Not on your face, is it? Or on top of your head?"

Odelia laughed out loud now. "No, Dooley, a baby bump doesn't suddenly show up on a person's face. It's actually right here," she said, and pleasantly patted her belly.

Dooley and I, who had the pleasure of riding shotgun, closely studied our human's belly. "I don't see any bump," said Dooley, and he seemed extremely relieved. All this talk of bumps had him worried, and me, too, I have to admit. It can't be a lot of fun to suddenly develop strange bumps where no bumps were before.

"That's because it's still early days," said Odelia. "It should start to show in a couple of weeks."

"How big does this bump get?" asked Dooley.

"Yes," I chimed in. "Are we talking a tennis-ball bump or a volleyball bump?"

"That depends," said Odelia. "Though I hope it won't be too big. I'd like to keep on working for as long as I can."

"What do you mean?" asked Dooley, a slight hint of panic clear in his voice. "You'll have to stop working because of the bump?"

"In the last couple of days or weeks I might have to take it easy," Odelia explained. "To make sure the baby is fine, and me, too."

Dooley gulped some more. His eyes had gone wide. "You mean having a baby… is dangerous?!"

"It is a delicate time for a woman, Dooley. So I might have to rest a lot." She tickled my friend under the chin. "But don't you worry. I'm sure everything will be just fine."

But Dooley didn't seem convinced, and as he stared some more at Odelia's as-yet non-existent bump, I could tell that her words had done little to assuage his concerns.

We'd arrived at a nice house in a cozy neighborhood, and Odelia parked her car right across the street. A big tree dominated the front yard, and judging from the house itself, the family that lived there took great care in maintaining their pleasant little home.

We walked up to the front door, and Odelia took a deep breath, then pressed her finger to the bell.

"Why did we have to come all the way out here?" I asked. "Why couldn't Mrs. Careen come to us?"

"Because Kristina Careen is agoraphobic, that's why," said Odelia. And when both Dooley and I stared at her, she explained, "She's afraid to go outside."

And she probably would have said more, but at that moment the door opened and a smallish woman with short blond hair appeared, and so we all stepped into the house.

Mrs. Careen quickly closed the door, as if afraid that some monster would reach inside and grab her if she left the door open for too long, and we followed her into the living room. Airy and bright, there were plenty of plants spread out throughout the roomy space, and there was even a grand piano near the window. On top of the piano, a veritable smorgasbord of framed pictures had been placed. I saw plenty of pictures of our hostess, out and about in many different places. Clearly Kristina Careen hadn't always been afraid to leave the house.

"Please take a seat," said our hostess, gesturing to a white leather couch. "Can I get you anything? Tea? Coffee?" She glanced down at me and Dooley. "Milk for the cats?"

"Water for the cats will be fine, and for me, too," said Odelia, taking a seat.

Mrs. Careen disappeared into the kitchen for a moment, and soon returned. "I'm sorry for dragging you out here," she said as she placed a large glass of cool water on a coaster on the coffee table, and a dish of the same on the floor for us. "But like I explained over the phone, I don't get out much." She grimaced. "Or rather, I don't get out at all these days."

"That's fine," said Odelia. "You said something about your daughter?"

"Yes," said Mrs. Careen, and picked up a framed picture of a fair-haired child and handed it to Odelia. "That's Poppy. She would have turned twenty this year."

"Would have?"

"She died thirteen years ago. Hit-and-run accident on the street in front of the house. She and her brother both. Rick survived, but Poppy didn't. Police say she died on impact. She didn't suffer." She sniffled. "At least there's that."

"I'm so sorry," said Odelia with feeling, as she reached out a hand to the woman.

Poppy's mother took Odelia's hand and pressed it gratefully. "The day Poppy died was the last day I set foot outside this house. For some reason I haven't been able to go out ever since. Psychologists say it's not uncommon for people suffering a great trauma to have lasting damage. But in my case it's extra hard, since my husband not only lost his daughter that day, he also lost his wife—or at least he lost part of me—and so did I."

"Did they ever catch who did it?"

"No, and that's what I wanted to talk to you about. I've been working closely with a therapist for years, and we've come to the conclusion that I'll never be able to work through this issue as long as there's no resolution to what happened to my little girl." She directed a hopeful look at Odelia, and scooted a little forward on the couch. "You see, the police interviewed a number of suspects, and their investigation focused on five men in particular. Five young men who were out joyriding that night, tearing through the neighborhood. One of those five men killed Poppy, and I want him identified and brought to justice. And maybe then I'll be able to be healed—and so will my husband and son."

"They're not here?"

"No, both Dominic and Rick are foresters. I'm also a forester, but for obvious reasons I haven't been able to work for the last thirteen years. And I must say I miss it terribly."

"You and your husband used to work together?"

She smiled and nodded. "Yes. That's how we met, actually. In the beginning we were colleagues. Our work was our passion—still is. And our passion for foresting gradually turned into a passion for each other, too. But while I developed this phobia, Dominic started distancing himself from me. We're still married, but our family got broken that day, and I'm hoping that by bringing Poppy's killer to justice, I can heal my family, too."

"So who do you think killed Poppy, Mrs. Careen?"

"Kristina, please." She took out a manila folder and opened it. Out spilled a number of press articles and photos. She spread out five of the photos on the coffee table. "These are the five men," she said, her expression hardening. "One of them killed my daughter, and has been able to get away with murder for the past thirteen years. But no more."

Obviously Kristina Careen felt very strongly about bringing the person responsible for her daughter's death to justice, and I didn't blame her. It was a horrible thing to do: first to kill a little girl and then to flee the scene of the crime and decide not to take responsibility for the terrible hurt you've caused.

"So who are these five men?" asked Odelia as she studied the pictures, picking them up one by one.

"Five friends," said Kristina. "As the police informed us at the time they were five spoiled rich kids, racing around in the expensive cars their rich daddies bought them. They were inseparable, and even though the police leaned on them, and their families, they all closed ranks and claimed they had nothing to do with what happened."

"Any witnesses?"

"Only Rick. But he was six at the time, and his testimony wasn't deemed reliable. Also, he'd been mowed down alongside his sister, and was lucky to come out of the incident with his life. As it was, he spent weeks in hospital, and still walks with a limp."

"Do they still live around here, these men?" asked Odelia.

"I've checked, and they do. I have to warn you, though, that three of them have filed a restraining order against me and my husband and my son. You see, we've been keeping tabs on them, determined that they won't be allowed to get away with their crime." She tapped the pictures. "Only one of them might be my daughter's killer, but as far as I'm concerned, they're all guilty for the crime of covering up the murder."

"You think they know who did it?"

"Of course they do. Absolutely."

"I only recognize this man," said Odelia, picking up a picture of a blond-haired beefy fellow. "Sergio Sorbet."

"Yes, Sergio is a big star now," said Kristina, contempt clear in her voice. "He was the first one to take out a restraining order. I kept writing to his agent and the movie studio. Warning them about the kind of man he is. Of course they never wrote back."

"Who's Sergio Sorbet, Max?" asked Dooley.

"He's a big action star," I said. "Famous for the Zeus movies."

"Zeus? Like the god Zeus?"

"Yeah, the god of thunder and lightning. Sergio plays Zeus, and his movies have grossed billions of dollars since he put that particular franchise on the map."

"So he's a movie star and also a child killer?"

"Possibly."

Kristina had taken out more manila folders and placed them all on the table. "I have extensive information about all of these men," she said. "You're welcome to go through it. That's Omar Wissinski. He runs an insurance agency with Jona Morro. Then there's Sergio, of course, and also Joel Timperley."

"Timperley? Doesn't his family own the Keystone Mall?"

"They do. They also own Timpermart—the supermarket chain. And finally there's Dunc Hanover—the artist."

"I think I've interviewed him once," said Odelia, picking up the man's picture. He had a crazy mane of hair and looked exactly like what one would expect an artist to look like: wild-eyed, frizzy-haired and a little unkempt.

"He's got a shop in his friend Joel's mall," said Kristina. "In fact they're all located at the mall. Wissinski and Morro have their insurance business set up at the mall, as well."

"And Sergio?"

"He's in town for the premiere of his latest movie, which is to take place—"

"At the Keystone Mall. So they're all here?"

"All of them. They never left. Shameless."

"Do you remember which police officer was in charge of the case?"

"Your uncle handled it personally. Which is how I arrived at you."

Odelia smiled. "You think I'll do a better job than my uncle?"

Kristina shrugged. "Chief Lip did his best, but if you've got five people who all clam up and then their families, who are amongst the wealthiest in Hampton Cove, all put up a wall around their sons… There wasn't anything he could do."

"They never found the car?"

She shook her head. "Disappeared. And no witnesses, either."

"Look, I'm not going to lie to you, Kristina. I'm not sure if I'll succeed where my uncle failed. I mean, if it was impossible to finger the person responsible for Poppy's death thirteen years ago, it will be even harder today. Evidence will have disappeared, witnesses won't remember or will have died…"

"I know. But I've heard so many good things about you."

She leaned forward and placed a hand on Odelia's knee. "You're smart, Mrs. Kingsley, and inventive. If anyone can find out what happened, it's you."

"I appreciate the vote of confidence," said Odelia softly. She'd picked up Poppy's picture again. The blond-haired angel's joy spat from the snap, and it was hard to imagine anyone would mow her down then think they could get away with it.

"Just give it your best shot," said Kristina. "That's all I'm asking."

"All right," said Odelia finally. "At the very least I can talk to these five men. Maybe in the years that have passed since that night they have developed a conscience."

Kristina scoffed, "I very much doubt that. But I've heard rumors of a falling-out, and I'm hoping that finally someone will be prepared to break rank." Her expression turned hard again. "Someone willing to finally own up to what they did to my little girl."

CHAPTER 3

Our next port of call were the woods that spread out just outside Hampton Cove. They're a popular place for weekend ramblers to go for hikes, and also for mountain bikers to practice their biking skills. It was a novel idea for us to realize that there were actually people taking care of those woods and that they were called foresters. I'd always thought that woods sort of took care of themselves somehow, but apparently they didn't.

We found Kristina's husband Dominic and their son Rick near the cabin they worked out of. We arrived there just in time, for they were on the verge of going out and entering the woods that were their domain. As Dominic explained it, they were going to fell some trees that had become dangerous and were on the verge of toppling over. Why that was a bad thing became clear when Dooley and I glanced up at one of those tall trees. Next to it, the forester's jeep was parked, and I could see how that tree could easily do a lot of damage to that jeep if it ever decided to give up the ghost and keel over.

Trees are big, you see, and in comparison cars are small. And if a person were to sit in that car when that tree came down, it would be game over for tree, car, and person!

"I just talked to your wife," Odelia explained her visit, "and she asked me to investigate the five men she thinks are responsible for your daughter's death."

Dominic's face spelled storm, I could tell. He had one of those bearded faces which seem to be all the rage with people who spend a lot of time in nature. Even his son Rick sported an impressive beard. Both men were dressed in sturdy boots, khaki pants, check shirts and were clearly very muscular and of the rugged, silent type. "I told my wife not to talk to you, but of course she had to go ahead and do it anyway," the forester grunted.

"She said she hopes that bringing Poppy's killer to justice might help her conquer her fear of open spaces."

"Lot of psycho-babble," the man grumbled.

"No, it's not, Dad," said Rick. "This all started the day Poppy died, and if Mom believes that finding her killer will help her, I think we must give her that chance, don't you think?"

"What I think clearly doesn't make any difference," said the man, staring off into the middle distance with a dark frown on what was visible of his face through the hirsute shrubbery.

"Do you remember anything from that day, Rick?" asked Odelia.

"Nothing much," said Rick. "All I remember is two cars coming at us at great speed. Poppy and I were playing. I was on my bike, and she was scribbling something on the street with chalk, when suddenly these cars came roaring up out of nowhere. I was lucky that I was on the bike. The car hit my bicycle from the side. It lifted me up and I was catapulted onto the sidewalk, where a tree broke my fall. But Poppy wasn't so lucky."

"Doctors told us that she broke every bone in her body," Dominic grunted. "Said they'd never seen anything like it. The car that hit her must have been doing ninety miles an hour. Which is why I refuse to call it an accident. It was cold-blooded murder, pure and simple." His voice broke as the memory of that day came back to him.

"I was in the hospital for the next couple of weeks," said Rick, placing a comforting arm around his dad's shoulder. "I remember the police questioning me a couple of times, but I couldn't tell them more than what I'm telling you now."

"Two dark cars."

He nodded. "Big and dark. But of course to a six-year-old every car looks big."

"I should never have left them outside to play," said Dominic. "But it was a safe neighborhood. Almost no traffic. Except for that one day when…" He swallowed.

"It's all right, Dad. It wasn't your fault, or Mom's. It was those crazy kids."

"Joyriders," said Odelia.

"Yeah, they'd been terrorizing other neighborhoods before that night," said Dominic. "The police were keeping an eye out for them, so they decided to move to our neighbor-hood, where they knew the police wouldn't be watching and waiting."

"What happened after that night?"

"They were all picked up—all five of them—and ques-tioned. But they closed ranks. And of course their daddies paid for the very best lawyers money can buy. In the end the police had to let them go. Couldn't prove a thing."

"And the car had disappeared."

"Yeah, they never did find the car that hit my kids. It's

probably at the bottom of a lake somewhere, or shipped off to God knows where."

"Do you think you'll be able to do anything, Mrs. Kingsley?" asked Rick.

"I don't know, Rick. But at the very least I'm going to talk to those men again."

"Good luck," Dominic scoffed. "We tried talking to them over the years, and you know what their answer was?"

"A restraining order, your wife told me."

Dominic nodded. "They were rotten kids, who have turned into rotten adults."

"Do you think they'll still cover for each other?"

"Of course they will. That kind of person doesn't change."

"Your wife seems to think they fell out. So at least one of them might talk."

"My wife is desperate, Mrs. Kingsley," said Dominic, squarely facing Odelia. "It's thirteen years she's been confined to that house. It's been hell on her—and us."

We'd almost reached the car when Dominic caught up with us. He glanced back, but Rick had disappeared inside the cabin they used as their GHQ. "There's something else you need to know," Kristina's husband said quietly.

"What is it?" asked Odelia.

"It's my wife. She was recently diagnosed with cancer. The doctors have given her three months—at best."

"Oh, God."

Dominic glowered at the forest floor. "She's hoping that before she dies, she'll know that the animal who killed our little girl is finally made to pay for what he did." He looked up. "Please don't tell Rick. We haven't told him yet. We're hoping for some miracle. And in case she recovers, we don't want to burden Ricky if it isn't absolutely necessary."

"Of course. I'm so sorry, Dominic."

He nodded. "Please do your best, Mrs. Kingsley."

"I will," Odelia said, much impressed. "You have my word."

CHAPTER 4

Jona Morro was grinning to himself as he studied a YouTube video on his phone. It was a demo from the new *High-Speed Chaser* game and looked really sick. It was only out next month, but Jona had a buddy who worked for the company that produced the game, and he'd been able to lay his hands on a copy three weeks before the official premiere. A real coup, and he was looking forward to spending all weekend playing on his computer.

He was behind his desk at Morro & Wissinski, the insurance company he and his buddy Omar had started years ago. And he was so engrossed in the preview that he didn't even hear it when someone walked up behind him and suddenly gave him such a knock on the head that immediately he conked out, his phone dropping to the floor.

When he finally woke up again, he was suffering from a terrible headache. But that was not the worst part. He was strapped to his desk, and found himself looking up at the huge car he'd once had hauled up to the ceiling and which now hung there, suspended.

It was the first car he'd ever owned. A red Ferrari. Every

single customer who walked into his office was impressed at the sight of that phenomenal car hanging over the desk. And all of them asked the same question: 'Oh, Mr. Morro! Isn't that dangerous?' And every single time he answered them the same thing, 'Not as dangerous as driving it was!'

In actual fact there wasn't any danger in having a car hanging over your head at all, at least if you trusted the people who'd rigged it up there with powerful steel cables.

Only as he slowly regained consciousness, he suddenly realized that those powerful steel cables were making strange noises. The same kind of noises a suspension bridge makes. That loud twanging couldn't be good! Nor could that terrible banging sound!

He now saw that the bolts that fastened the cables to the wall had been loosened, and the car was now suspended above him with only a single bolt! And as he glanced over, he suddenly became aware of the terrible danger he was in.

"Hey, are you crazy? Stop that!" he cried as he watched a sledgehammer pound the final remaining bolt that kept the Ferrari from crushing him. "Stop that right now!"

Suddenly, the bolt gave way and was torn from the wall. There was one final twang, then the car came crashing down.

CHAPTER 5

The first people Odelia decided to talk to were Jona Morro and Omar Wissinski. They had both filed a restraining order against Kristina's family, so she reasoned they were the ones with the most to hide—and the most likely suspects in that fatal hit and run.

But when we arrived there the place was in turmoil for some reason, with police everywhere.

The firm of Morro & Wissinski was located in a corridor that forked off the main atrium of the Keystone Mall in Hampton Keys. The mall serves Hampton Cove, Hampton Keys and Happy Bays, and has been a popular mainstay in these parts for many decades. For obvious reasons I haven't been there a lot—cats don't like to do their own shopping, leaving the carrying of those heavy bags of cat kibble and cat litter to their loving owners. The parking lot was pretty much full, indicating that the mall was as popular as ever. And when we entered, the atrium was a sight to behold: a large display of *Zeus: Tempter of Fate* was in obvious evidence. The new Zeus movie was having its Long Island premiere at the mall this weekend, and they had pulled out all the stops. Life-sized figures of Zeus and his main nemesis Dr. Ghoul had been placed there, surrounded by props depicting a scene from the movie, where clearly Zeus was fighting the good fight against his eternal enemy.

"Very impressive," Dooley said as he watched the display with awe. Around us, young kids were also looking their eyes out, they being the main audience for the Zeus franchise, and presumably every other motion picture that comes out of Hollywood these days.

"I wonder how we'll be able to talk to this Sergio Sorbet guy," I said. "If he's as big a star as this display tells me he is, he'll have agents and minders and assistants and lawyers and bodyguards, all of them shielding him from a woman determined to find out if he drove the car that killed Poppy."

"Odelia will find a way," said Dooley as we trudged on in our human's wake. "She always does."

"Yeah, she is tenacious," I agreed. "And she can always play the pregnancy card."

"The pregnancy card?"

"Yeah, when they try to throw her out, or things get rough, she can point to her belly and demand that they treat a pregnant woman with the respect she deserves."

"She can tell them about her baby lump. I'm sure they'll be impressed."

"Baby bump, Dooley, not lump."

And we would have entered the offices of Morro & Wissinski, if not a beefy and serious-looking police officer stood parked in front, clearly put there to keep people out.

"What's going on?" asked Odelia.

"Robbery," the man said, then lowered his voice. "One of them got a car dropped on top of him, if you can believe it!"

"A car dropped on top of him?" asked Odelia, looking at the man as if he'd gone nuts.

"Better take a look," the cop advised, and stepped aside to allow Odelia in. She was, after all, a colleague of his.

You see, Odelia is a reporter, but she's also a civilian consultant attached to the police department, and as such even has the badge to prove it.

Once inside, we quickly saw what the cop at the door had meant: a very large car had been dropped on top of a desk. The desk had collapsed under the weight of the car, which must have weighed a ton—literally—and I could see an arm poking from between the car and what was left of the desk. On the floor, a pool of blood indicated that the man hadn't survived the incident.

"Hey, babe," suddenly a voice sounded. "What brings you here?"

We glanced up, and found ourselves looking into the smiling face of Odelia's husband Chase. The burly cop was donning plastic gloves, and now handed similar gloves to our human. He was dressed in his usual outfit: jeans, boots and a white T-shirt stretched taut over a muscular torso. His dark hair almost reached his shoulders. Chase never did enjoy visiting the hairdresser.

"Is that…" Odelia said, pointing to the dead man.

"Jona Morro," said Chase, his smile vanishing.

Next to the car wreck, a man was poking around, trying to get a good look at the body. It was hard, since the car was blocking his view. The man was Abe Cornwall, our county coroner, and he clearly resented having to work under these circumstances.

"What have you got for us, Abe?" asked Chase.

"Well, he's dead, I'm afraid," said Abe.

"Don't tell me. Death by car crash?"

"Something like that." The paunchy coroner looked up. "From what I understand this car used to be suspended up there, hanging from the ceiling."

"So an accident, you think?"

"I doubt it. Look at this."

We all looked where the coroner was pointing. A sledge-hammer stood leaning against the door.

"Someone knocked the supporting bolts out of the wall, causing the car to drop down on top of the fellow." He now gestured to his crew of crime scene technicians, who all looked like Martians, in their CSI gear. "Can someone get this car out of here!" Abe said.

"Weird way to kill a person," said Chase.

"I thought it was a robbery?" said Odelia as we stepped into the next office. Here a man sat, nursing a cup of coffee and looking white as a sheet. His head was bandaged and I had a feeling this just might be the Wissinski of Morro & Wissinski fame.

"Oh, it was. Knocked out this poor bastard, emptied the safe, and killed the other guy."

"Is that Wissinski?"

"Yep, that's him. I was just going to take his statement. Care to join me?"

"I actually came here to talk to him—him and his partner."

"What about?"

"Both of them were probably involved in a historic hit-and-run case that killed a little girl. The mother asked me to take a look at the case, and hopefully identify the driver."

"And you think Wissinski and Morro were involved?"

"They were both part of a group of men who were picked up that night. They'd been out joyriding, and one of them must have driven the car that hit Poppy Careen."

"Careen," said Chase, frowning. "Name doesn't seem to ring a bell."

"That's because it happened thirteen years ago."

"And they never caught the guy?"

"Nope. And it destroyed that family."

"I can imagine."

They both studied Wissinski, who tried to bring the plastic cup of coffee to his lips with shaking hands, then finally managed to take a sip.

"Mr. Wissinski?" said Chase, stepping up to the guy.

The insurance broker looked up. "Yes?"

"I'd like to take your statement now, sir."

"But I already told your colleague everything."

"I know, but sometimes more details spring to mind a second time." He'd taken out his notebook and held his pencil poised. "So can you tell me what happened here, sir?"

Mr. Wissinski swallowed. "I was on the phone with a client when two men walked in."

"Description?"

"One was tall, the other short. They were wearing black masks. Immediately one of them took out a gun and pointed it at me. Said he wanted me to open the safe for him."

"What did the gun look like?"

"Just… a handgun, I guess? I'm no expert," he added apologetically.

"Go on."

"I led the man with the gun to the safe, and opened it. Then suddenly I heard a loud crash, but before I could look over, he hit me over the head and I fell down. When I came to, the safe was empty, the men were gone, and when I staggered back into the office, I saw that Jona…" He gulped a little, and I could see the terror in his eyes as he pictured the scene in his mind's eye. "Jona was…"

"I understand," said Chase. "Jona Morro was your partner?"

"Yes, we started this business together."

"Why do you think they killed him?"

"I have no idea," said Mr. Wissinski with a helpless shrug.

"Do you think they had some kind of beef with him?"

"It's possible, I guess."

"Did you recognize the men?"

"No, I've never seen them before."

"But it's possible that Mr. Morro knew them."

"Yes, we each kept our own list of clients."

"So when a new client walked in…"

"We divvied them up on an equal basis."

"I see." Chase jotted down a few notes, while Mr. Wissinski looked on, deeply impressed by the whole business. "Lot of valuables in the safe?"

"Some money, some securities we kept for some of our clients."

"Very daring robbery," said Chase, as he fixed the man with a steely gaze. "In broad daylight. Do you have a camera in the office?"

"No, unfortunately we don't. I've told Jona many times we should have one installed, but he didn't like the idea. Said it would scare away potential customers. You see, we get a lot of wealthy clients in here—and they're very attached to their privacy."

"I will need an inventory of what was taken. And I'd like you to work with a sketch artist for the robbers. I've checked and there is an extensive security system in the mall, so we should be able to pick them out of the crowd as they were entering and leaving the office."

"Thank you, Mr. Kingsley," said the insurance man as he shook Chase's hand with quaking fingers. Obviously the man was completely undone, and it wasn't hard to see why.

"And now my wife would like to ask you a couple of questions, if you don't mind, Mr. Wissinski," said Chase.

"Oh, of course."

"This is actually not connected with the robbery," said

Odelia. "I don't know if you remember Mrs. Careen—Mrs. Kristina Careen?"

Omar Wissinski shook his head. "Not again with the hit-and-run business."

"Kristina Careen seems to believe that you and your friends had something to do with the death of her daughter," said Odelia. "Is there anything you can tell me about what happened that day?"

"No, nothing," said the insurance man, giving her a sad look. "Look, I said all I had to say ten years ago."

"Thirteen," Odelia corrected him gently.

"I wasn't there. None of us were. We were all questioned, and questioned again, and finally the police had to admit we had nothing to do with the whole business. I don't know who killed that little girl, Mrs. Kingsley. I know it wasn't me. And I feel terrible for the parents. But hounding us won't do them any good."

"You filed a restraining order against the Careens?"

"I had to. Dominic Careen kept harassing us. Calling us, showing up here, showing up at my house… Finally I just couldn't take it anymore and so I made sure he kept away from me. That man is a forester, Mrs. Kingsley. He chops wood for a living. And once he showed up here wielding a very big ax, threatening us."

"What did he say?"

"That if we didn't confess he'd make us."

"But the police have determined that you were joyriding that night."

"I'm not denying that. But we were nowhere near the place where that girl died."

"So you think it must have been another person, unrelated to you and your friends?"

"Yes."

He looked on the verge of a breakdown, and I think Odelia must have noticed, too, for she decided to leave the man be for now. After all, he'd just had a nasty conk on the head.

"Thank you for your time, Mr. Wissinski," she said therefore.

"Look, I feel sorry for the Careens, I really do, but I had nothing to do with the accident, I swear."

Just then, loud voices interrupted us. They seemed to come from the front of the shop, and when we went over to look what was going on, we saw that a man tried to gain access but was being held back by the same cop who'd allowed us to pass through.

The man didn't look happy, and when he caught sight of Omar, he shouted, "I want my money back, you thief! Give me back my money right now—or else!"

He wasn't wielding an ax, like Dominic had done, but he looked dangerous enough!

CHAPTER 6

The shouting man turned out to be answering to the name Gene Stooge, and when Chase took him apart, he was already less belligerent. Chase has that effect on people.

"So what seems to be the problem?" asked Chase.

"That man," said Mr. Stooge, pointing an accusatory finger at Omar Wissinski, "robbed my mother of her savings."

"I did nothing of the kind," said Omar, shaking his head, then seemed to get a little woozy, and decided that keeping his head perfectly still was probably the better option.

"He came in and made my mom all kinds of promises about doubling her money if she decided to invest with them and instead her money is now gone—all of it!"

"Your mother's money isn't gone at all, I can assure you," said Omar, then frowned. "Though now that I come to think of it…"

"See!" the irate customer shouted. "He's admitting it!"

"We just had a robbery," Omar explained. "And I'm afraid your mother's money was in the safe, along with that of some of our other customers."

"You robbed us!"

"No, we were robbed."

The man made a throwaway gesture with his hand, then turned to Chase. "Can I file a complaint with you, officer?"

"What did your mother invest in, sir?" asked Odelia.

"Some bitcoin nonsense," said Mr. Stooge.

"It isn't nonsense," said Omar adamantly. "Our bitcoin fund is a high-yield investment and is doing very well indeed."

"So why did the paper say that bitcoin is one big scam?"

"Why do you believe anything that's written in the papers?"

Dooley and I glanced to Odelia, whose face had flushed a little. Still she decided to keep her tongue. Now was not the time to defend her professional honor.

"So you advised Mr. Stooge's mother to invest in your bitcoin fund?" she asked instead.

"I advise all of our customers to invest in our bitcoin fund. It's the fund of the future. And it wouldn't surprise me if it will be our most successful fund ever. But like with all high-yield investments there is a certain level of risk involved."

"When I called you yesterday and asked for my mother's money back you said she had signed a contract and you wouldn't give it back!" the angry customer cried.

"I explained all this to Leta, Gene. When you invest in the bitcoin fund you invest for the long term. If everyone took out their money a week into their investment we'd never be able to turn a profit. It's the way we've always worked here at Morro & Wissinski."

"Ah, nuts," the man grumbled, clearly not satisfied with this explanation. "I wish my mother would have told me before she gave you all of her savings."

"Trust me, Gene," said the insurance man. "You stand to double your investment. Maybe even triple it."

"I thought you just said the money's been stolen?" said Chase.

Omar seemed to slump a little as this sobering truth came home to him. "Oh, darn it," he muttered, then closed his eyes and seemed to sway, like a sapling in the breeze.

"I think you better go home, Mr. Wissinski," Odelia suggested. "You don't look so good."

"I think you better go to the hospital," said Chase, eyeing the man with a worried frown. "You might have a concussion, sir."

"You're right," said Wissinski as he got up, then abruptly sat down again. And right before our eyes, his eyes suddenly turned up in his skull, and he would have crashed down onto the floor, if Chase hadn't been there to catch him.

"We better call an ambulance," said Odelia.

"Yeah, looks like he got hit harder than he thought."

"So what's going to happen with my money?" asked Gene Stooge.

"I thought it was your mother's money?" said Chase dryly.

"Is he going to pay me back or not?" the man demanded, pointing to the unconscious insurance broker.

"Please go home, Mr. Stooge," said Chase. "Now is not the time."

"I should have known," Gene grumbled as he got up. "It's all Jona's fault. He's the one who's behind this scheme, isn't he?"

"What makes you say that?" asked Odelia.

"Because it's true! Everybody knows that Jona is the one who handles the investments, while Omar handles the insurance side of the business." He planted both feet firmly on the floor. "I demand to speak to Jona. Right now!"

"I'm afraid that's not possible," said Chase.

"And why not? Are you protecting that crook?"

"Because Jona Morro is dead, Gene, that's why."

Once Gene Stooge had finally left the scene, after much grumbling, and Omar Wissinski had been taken to a nearby hospital, a crashing noise alerted us of a great work being carried out in the inner office. When we looked over, the car that had killed Jona Morro had finally been lifted from the poor man's body. And I have to say that the sight of the guy wasn't pleasing to the eye. He looked… flattened. And very dead indeed.

"Cause of death is pretty obvious, I guess?" said Chase.

But Abe was too busy examining the dead man to respond. Finally he said, "As far as I can tell he was hit over the head, then tied to his desk. The blow must have knocked him out cold."

"Was he conscious when the car fell on top of him?"

"Hard to tell. He could have been. Which would make this a pretty gruesome way to go." He directed a cross look at Chase, as if holding him personally responsible for the poor man's death. "I'll be able to tell you more later. But I have to hand it to you, Chase. This is probably the first time I've ever seen a man killed in quite this fashion."

"Hey, I didn't do it, Abe!" said Chase.

"Hm," said Abe, then addressed a member of his staff. "You can take him away now."

And since there wasn't anything keeping us there, we decided to take our leave as well.

"Odd, isn't it, Max?" said Dooley as we followed Odelia out of the office.

"What is, Dooley?" I asked.

"We came here looking for a man who killed a little girl in a hit and run, and we find a man who's been killed in a hit and run."

"Yeah, only this hit and run is a little special."

"Still—it's a big coincidence, don't you think?"

"Yeah, a bit too much of a coincidence, if you ask me."

CHAPTER 7

We were in Odelia's uncle's office, where the Chief was discussing the case with his niece and Chase.

"Strange business," Uncle Alec grunted as he pensively fingered the third of his chins. "One man knocked out cold, the other one crushed with his own car…" He turned to Chase. "Security caught these guys on CCTV?"

"Nope. Turns out there's CCTV in the mall, but it doesn't cover every single nook and cranny. And Morro & Wissinski is one of the businesses that aren't covered."

"Did they at least catch the robbers as they fled the scene?"

"Nope. The camera covering the particular section of the mall where Morro & Wissinski are located is broken. Has been broken for weeks and should have been fixed but hasn't."

"What are the chances the robbers knew?"

Chase shrugged. "We looked for them on the other feeds, but so far we've got nothing."

"It's a daring heist, to be sure," said the Chief.

"I don't know. That part of the mall isn't exactly bustling,

Chief. They've put plenty of the same kinds of businesses together: banks, insurance agencies, real estate offices..."

"I see. So not as much foot traffic as other parts."

"I wonder if this robbery is connected to the hit and run I've been asked to investigate," said Odelia.

"Oh, right. The Poppy Careen case," said her uncle. He shook his head. "Sad business. I remember it well. Very frustrating that we never found the lunatic who killed that girl."

"The Careens seem convinced that it must have been one of five men," said Odelia. "And two of those men were targeted in the robbery this morning."

"Yeah, I'm not so sure the Careens are right. We never managed to find any evidence placing the men they accused in their neighborhood that night. We did find several witness statements linking them to another hit and run in a different part of town the week before. Luckily no one got injured, though they did cause a lot of damage to the house they rammed."

"They rammed a house?"

Uncle Alec nodded. "Drove straight in through the front door. Lucky for them no one was home at the time, but the structure all but collapsed. Had to be completely rebuilt."

"Did you ever confront them with the accusations leveled at them by the Careens?"

"Oh, absolutely. Seeing as we didn't pick up any other joyriders that night, it seemed likely it must have been them. But there were no witnesses placing them at the scene, and once the little boy woke up—"

"Rick Careen."

"—he couldn't tell us a lot more either."

"So how did Kristina and her husband arrive at these five kids?"

"Well, like I said, they were the only ones caught joyriding that night. And also, there had been plenty of complaints on

33

previous nights. And on one of those nights they'd come close to the street where Poppy Careen was killed. Two blocks, if I remember correctly. Which was all the Careens needed to blame them for the death of their daughter."

"And what do you think, Uncle Alec? You talked to them. Do you think one of those five men killed Poppy?"

"It's possible," her uncle admitted. "But without any evidence, my hands were tied."

"What are the chances that Dominic Careen is one of the men who robbed Morro & Wissinski?" said Chase. "He clearly has a grudge against the two men. So what if he and his wife decided that it must have been Jona Morro who killed Poppy? And so after waiting all those years in vain they finally decided to take justice into their own hands and killed Morro? I mean, the way he died speaks volumes, don't you think?"

"Is it possible that the car that killed Morro is the same car that killed Poppy Careen?" asked Uncle Alec. "Can you look into that, Chase?"

"I doubt it," said Chase. "The guy would be an idiot to string up a car used in a hit and run."

"From what I hear, Jona Morro was a pretty cocky fellow. And as I remember, all five of those kids were convinced they could do whatever they wanted and get away with it. So maybe Morro decided to string up that car as a statement."

"Statement of what?" asked Chase.

"To tell the world: you can't touch me. I'm above the law."

"If he's the guy that killed Poppy, his crime finally caught up with him."

"I'll have another chat with Kristina and Dominic," said Odelia.

"And this time I'm coming with you," said Chase, and he wasn't taking no for an answer.

"Do you think that Dominic and Rick Careen are the two

men who killed Jona Morro and knocked out Omar Wissinski, Max?" asked Dooley.

"I don't know, Dooley, but it certainly warrants looking into."

"If they did kill Mr. Morro, do you think the judge will be very lenient with them? They did what the police couldn't do, after all: find justice for Poppy."

"It's not up to ordinary citizens to go out and kill people, Dooley. What if Jona Morro had nothing to do with Poppy's death? Then the wrong person was killed today."

"But what if it was him?"

"Then they should have told Odelia what kind of evidence they had, and she could have done something about it."

"Poor Odelia," said Dooley, as he studied our human. "Maybe we should tell her to stay home and rest. She is pregnant, after all. It's not good for the baby, Max. She's putting herself at risk."

"I think you'll find that it's very hard for anyone to stop Odelia from doing exactly what she wants to do, Dooley. Not even us."

"Maybe Chase can talk to her? He is the baby's dad, after all. He should look after its health, and the health of its mother."

"I'm sure Odelia is fine," I said reassuringly. "And besides, Chase is with her. He'll watch out for her. And when he's not around, we are also there, Dooley. We can protect her."

A dangerous glint had come into Dooley's eyes. "This will be our mission from now on, Max. We'll protect Odelia and her baby with tooth and claw!"

"Um, okay," I said. "Though maybe less of the tooth and claw for now. A calm and soothing environment is also important for an expecting mother."

"Then she shouldn't go out and investigate murders, Max!"

And we were right back where we started. These circular arguments were a given with Dooley. Tough to convince him of anything. He kept returning to his original statement, no matter what I said. In that sense he was almost as stubborn as Odelia. Then again, we were her cats, after all. So maybe we took after her? Or did she take after us?

CHAPTER 8

We were back at the Careen place, only this time Dominic had joined his wife on the big couch, and son Rick stood behind it, as if reluctant to take a seat, lest he had to do a runner.

"It's a simple question, Mr. Careen," said Chase, who had taken the lead. "Did you or didn't you blame Jona Morro for the death of your daughter?"

Dominic's face spelled storm, but his wife did her best to be the peacekeeper. "Like I told Odelia this morning, we don't know which of the five friends killed Poppy. All we know is that one of them must be responsible."

"I knew it was Morro," said Rick suddenly.

His mother turned to him. "Rick!"

"It's all right, Mom. He's dead now. And good riddance, as far as I'm concerned."

"Why did you think it was Jona Morro?" asked Odelia.

"I asked around, and Morro used to visit the same club where I like to hang out a lot. He used to boast about his speed racing record. His family own a race car team, you see, and when he was young Jona wanted to become a race car driver. And he was pretty good, too. Said he loved racing, but what he loved even more was street racing. So one night he was boasting, and someone asked him why he'd stopped street racing, if he loved it so much. He said there had been an incident, and someone was killed, so his dad made him stop. From that moment he was only allowed to race on the track anymore, not the street." He shrugged. "It told me all I needed to know. He's the one who killed Poppy, all right."

"We can't be sure, Rick," said his mom. "He was just boasting."

"I don't think so. He was telling the truth."

"Why didn't you report this?" asked Chase.

"It would have been my word against his, wouldn't it? And that slippery bastard would have walked. Again."

"So you decided to take the law into your own hands, is that what you're saying?"

"Of course not. Though I have to say I'm not going to shed any tears over the guy."

"Rick, please," said his mom.

"No, Mom, I'm serious. I'm glad he's dead. He got exactly what he deserved."

"Where were you this morning between nine and ten?" asked Chase.

"You know where I was," said Dominic curtly. "In the woods. Your wife saw me there."

"My wife talked to you around ten-thirty," said Chase. "So where were you before then?"

"Not at the mall, if that's what you're implying," said the man, getting up. His weather-beaten face had taken on a darker shade of puce. Dominic Careen definitely had a temper.

"We were in the woods," said Rick. "My dad and me both."

"Can anyone confirm that?"

"I can confirm that my dad was there. And he can confirm that I was there. Isn't that enough?"

Chase grimaced. "Hardly. Two men knocked out Omar Wissinski this morning, emptied the safe, and killed Jona Morro by dropping a car on top of him. You can see how this raises a number of questions. Especially since it's not so easy to bring that car down. It requires a lot of physical strength, and a knowledge of how to work the steel cables that kept the car suspended. You're both foresters. You're well-equipped to handle such a job. Well-equipped, with the required know-how and experience plus motivation."

"Well, we didn't do it," said Dominic.

"I suggest you don't leave town, Mr. Careen," said Chase, getting up. "And that goes for you, too, Rick." And after fixing both men with a steely look, he left the room, leaving the three surviving members of the Careen family slightly reeling, I could tell.

But Chase was absolutely right, of course. This job had father and son Careen's signature written all over it. Kristina wanted Odelia to bring Poppy's killer to justice, but her husband and son had beaten her to it: they'd meted out that justice personally.

"So what do you think?" asked Odelia once we were back in the car. We could see the Careens glancing at us through the window and they did not look happy.

"It's them," said Chase. "It has to be. Who else would do such a thing? Any ordinary robber would have simply tied up both men and emptied that safe. They wouldn't have gone to the trouble of killing Jona Morro, and most definitely not by dumping his own car on top of him. No, it has to be them."

"You could always apply for a warrant and search the house," Odelia suggested. "If it was them they must have stashed the contents of that safe somewhere in the house."

"No, they're much too clever for that. They probably got

it somewhere in those woods. There must be hundreds of places where they could put that loot. Probably buried next to some tree. And when they figure the time is right, they'll start spending that money."

"I don't know, Chase. Killing Jona Morro is one thing, but stealing the money?"

"Why not? They must have figured that Morro owed them. For the life he took."

"It's possible," she conceded. "So what are you going to do now?"

"Now I keep a close eye on them. At some point they have to dig up the loot. And when they do, I'll nab them."

"You're going to put surveillance on them?"

"Oh, you bet I am."

"Honestly, Chase, don't you think the Careens have suffered enough? After all, Morro did kill their little girl. If he died by their hand, maybe they had a point?"

He turned to her with a frown. "Babe, no one should be allowed to take the law into their own hands. That way lies anarchy and chaos."

She sighed. "I guess you're right." She placed a surreptitious hand on her belly. Immediately Chase glanced down, a look of alarm on his face.

"Are you all right?"

"Oh, sure," she said with a grin. "Just force of habit, I guess."

"Maybe you shouldn't be involved in my cases from now on."

"Chase!" she said.

"At least until after the baby is born."

"God, babe, not you, too. My mom has been on my case, and so has my dad and Gran. And I'm going to tell you what I told them: if you expect me to stay home from now on until after the birth, you're crazy. I'm a working woman, and I'm going to keep on working for as long as I can. And there's absolutely nothing wrong with that!" she emphasized when Chase tried to interrupt her.

"I know there's nothing wrong with that, but please be careful, okay?"

She placed a loving hand on his arm. "I'm always careful. And besides, I have you to take care of me, don't I?"

"That, you have," said Chase, and they shared a kiss.

Though when Odelia wasn't looking, Chase gave her a look of concern.

Clearly the cop wasn't at ease with his wife traipsing around investigating murder cases!

CHAPTER 9

Mandi Gusta was in a good mood. Ever since her husband had taken over his dad's garage, business had been picking up with leaps and bounds. The old man was a great mechanic, and a genuinely nice guy, but he had no head for business, and he'd neglected to invest in the old garage he'd taken over from his own dad once upon a long time ago.

But Jefferson had passed away, and his son Vince was now in charge, and it seemed as if a new wind was blowing through the place. And since Mandi was in charge of the books, she had a front-row seat to the revival of the Gusta Garage, an established name in town.

So it was with a song on her lips that she closed up the shop and decided to head home. She still had some shopping to do, and pick up some dry-cleaning in town. And she was walking to her car, parked behind the shop, when the smell of acrid smoke irritated her nostrils and she frowned in confusion. Who had lit a fire on such a nice day?

And then she saw it: behind the garage, Vince was burning something in a metal vat that had stood there rusting for ages. As she approached, he walked away, though.

He was so lost in thought that he hadn't even noticed her. And since curiosity was her middle name, she decided to take a look at what her husband was so very eager to burn.

A bunch of old notebooks, she saw. And since she was the Gusta Garage bookkeeper, she decided it was her business to see what could possibly be in those notebooks.

Vince had once told her that his dad kept two accounts: an official one, and one for customers who preferred to pay him under the table. Nowadays the practice had been banned, but back in the day it had been standard for a lot of small business owners.

So she took a branch, and fished out one of the notebooks. It was leather-bound, and the fire hadn't yet had the chance to consume it. She opened it and started reading.

CHAPTER 10

That evening, dinner time at the Poole family soon turned into sleuth-night, as the only topic of conversation was the spectacular crime that had taken place at the mall.

The Pooles weren't the only family discussing the case, since the murder of Jona Morro had clearly gripped people's imagination. After all, it isn't every day that a murder takes place at the mall. And it isn't every day that people are killed with their own car.

"I think it must have been the Careens," said Gran. "They had the motive, the opportunity, and the means—and frankly speaking, I think they had the right, too!"

"Oh, Ma, for crying out loud," said Uncle Alec. "Nobody should be allowed to take the law into their own hands. If they think a crime has been committed—they should tell us!"

"They did tell you, and you screwed up, didn't you?"

"Anyone more sausages?" asked Tex, who loved the treat almost as much as I did. I know, I know. Sausages are more often associated with dogs, but why should they be the only ones who enjoy a nice sausage? Unfortunately, Tex ignored me completely. That's what you get for being overexcited about something. You set yourself up to be disappointed.

We were in Marge and Tex's backyard, which is well-equipped to cater to so many people: Odelia's parents were there, of course, but also Uncle Alec and his girlfriend Charlene, and Gran and her friend Scarlett.

"I don't think the Careens would ever do such a thing," said Charlene.

"You know them?" asked Odelia.

"Of course. Poor woman," said the Mayor. "Hasn't left that house in years. Let's hope that now that the murderer of her little girl is dead, she'll be able to overcome her ordeal."

"Her son told us that she doesn't have more than three months to live," said Odelia.

"Oh, no!" said Charlene, clasping her hands to her face. "Poor family!"

"Which is another reason for you not to bother them anymore, Mister," said Gran, waving a big knife in her son's face. "That family has suffered enough already."

"Ma, if they committed a crime, they have to do the time," the Chief said solemnly.

"All they did was mete out some much-needed justice!"

"We don't know that, do we? Jona Morro may be innocent of the crime they think he committed. All they had to go on was some gossip from some of his so-called friends."

"Well, I think you should leave well enough alone now, Alec Lip," Gran spoke sternly. "There's plenty of real criminals out there. Just leave the Careens be."

"What's all the fuss about?" asked Harriet, who was stretched out on the grass, right next to her mate Brutus.

And since it didn't look like that sausage was coming in my direction any time soon, I wandered over and plunked myself down next to them. And in a few short words I related the entire history to my two friends.

"Sad business," Harriet determined. "Though now that justice has been served, maybe the woman will feel better and won't succumb to the disease."

"Yeah, let's hope so," I said.

"I think she will be just fine," said Dooley, who had also joined us.

"So what's this business with the bitcoin?" asked Brutus.

"Yeah, that's what I'd like to know," said Harriet.

"Well, apparently Morro & Wissinski invest in bitcoin on behalf of their clients," I said. "Though the man we saw today didn't seem very happy about the investment."

"I looked into this bitcoin," said Harriet. "And it looks very promising. Did you know that an investment of a hundred dollars today can turn into millions tomorrow?"

"I don't know about that," I said. "To be honest it sounds more like a scam to me."

"Max! How can you say that! Bitcoin is the future."

"Of course it is," I said, and closed my eyes for a nap. If I wasn't getting a sausage, at least I could dream of sausages. It wasn't the same thing, but it was a close second.

"You know what we should do, snuggle bear?" asked Harriet.

"What, sugar biscuit?"

"Start our own bitcoin!"

"Can we do that?"

"Of course! Anyone can start a bitcoin. We'll call it… HarrietCoin."

"Or BrutusCoin?"

"HarrietCoin sounds better."

"I guess so."

"Now all we have to do is start a website that can accept money, and we're in business!"

"Don't these bitcoins have to be mined or something?" I asked, opening my eyes for a moment to see if Tex hadn't changed his mind and was coming our way bearing sausage.

"Oh, don't you worry about that," said Harriet with a gesture of her paw. "I looked into all of that today, and there's plenty of people who don't bother with the mining. Too much hassle. All they do is start a website, give it a fancy name, and start collecting money!"

"Won't these investors expect a return on their investment?"

"Are you kidding! Once you've collected enough money, you simply close up shop!"

"I think that's called fraud, Harriet," I pointed out. "And you will go to jail."

"No one would put a cat in jail, Max," she said laughingly.

"They might put Odelia in jail, since it's her computer you'll be using."

"Oh," said Harriet, and gave this some thought. Then finally she shrugged. "I guess I'm prepared to take that chance."

"Yeah, but will Odelia be prepared to take that chance?"

"If I make her enough money? Of course she will!"

Oh, brother.

Dooley had stretched himself out next to me, and while Harriet and Brutus were talking bitcoin—or HarrietCoin—my friend seemed to have other, more important matters on his mind. "When that baby comes, Max, do you think we'll still be allowed to sleep at the foot of the bed?"

"Of course."

"Because... I've heard that parents of babies stop sleeping, Max. They stay up all day and all night. And if Odelia and Chase don't sleep, we won't get any sleep either."

"Of course they sleep. Humans can't go without sleep, Dooley. They'd die."

"Die! Oh, no!"

"Which is exactly why they have to sleep. And they will. Sleep, I mean—not die."

"But I had it from a good source."

"What source?"

"Kingman. He said that parents of newborns never sleep."

"And how would Kingman know? His human doesn't have babies."

"Kingman knows everything, Max. It's uncanny."

Well, that's true enough, I suppose. Kingman does know a lot about a lot of things. "I'm sure that everything will be all right," I said, yawning and stretching.

Dooley didn't get the message, though, for he continued, "If they don't sleep, and don't allow us to sleep, we'll have to move in with Marge and Tex, Max."

"We don't have to move in with Marge and Tex."

"If we want to get some sleep, we'll have to move in with them. But Harriet and Brutus sleep at the foot of their bed. And so we'll have to sleep with Gran. But her bed is too small. There's no room for the both of us, so one of us will have to sleep on the couch." He gave me nervous glances. "We'll be split up, Max! We won't be together anymore!"

"We'll always be together, buddy," I said sleepily. "Maybe we can both sleep on the couch. How about that?"

His furry face lit up. "You think?"

"Of course. We'll sleep on Marge and Tex's couch. Until the baby is old enough. And then we'll move back to Odelia's bed again."

"Oh, Max," said my friend, giving me an impromptu hug. "You're so smart!"

And then I finally did nod off, and as I did, suddenly a bright idea occurred to me, and I was wide awake again.

Of course! Why didn't I think of that sooner!

CHAPTER 11

Kristina Careen wasn't exactly feeling on top of the world. When the police suddenly drop by and start accusing your husband and son of murder, the experience isn't an enjoyable one. She'd been trying to get the police to take an interest in their plight for over a decade, and now all of a sudden the police were showing an interest, but for all the wrong reasons!

She had breakfasted with Dominic and Rick, before they'd left for work, and now she had the house all to herself again, and she soon found herself relaxing to a slight degree. She was sipping from her cup of coffee and looking out across the street, with its passersby. The first wave of the day had passed, with its school kids and people hurrying to get to work, and now the second wave was about to start with people going shopping, delivery services delivering their wares, the postman doing his rounds, and plumbers, roofers and electricians arriving to fix the myriad things in a house that can go kaput.

In other words: a day like all others. There was a certain calm that came with the routine, a calm she'd come to appreciate. It soothed her nerves, and actually she preferred week-days over weekends. She liked the busyness of a regular day —the fixed routine.

So when the mail slot in the door rattled, she welcomed it like an old friend. When she went over to check, she saw that a thick brown envelope lay on the mat. She frowned, wondering what it could be. She hadn't ordered anything, and the only thing she could think of was that Rick had bought something online again. He was always buying stuff.

She opened the package and found a black leather-bound notebook inside. And when she opened it, she found lists of numbers and dates—names and strange scribblings. The notebook was charred at the edges, but its contents had been preserved by the sturdy leather covering. A little hand-written note had been added. It said: 'I thought this might be of interest to you. Make sure you check October 14. Good luck—a well-wisher.'

A little shock had run through her system at the mention of that particular date. It was the day after Poppy's death. She leafed through the notebook with nervous fingers, until she landed on the date mentioned by the 'well-wisher' and found herself staring at the entry. It took a moment for its signifi-cance to reveal itself to her, but when it finally did, she gasped, then immediately reached for her phone and dialed a now-familiar number.

"Odelia?" she said. "Can you come over? I have something you need to see."

CHAPTER 12

Odelia found the way to the Careens easily. Unlike the first time, she didn't even need her GPS. Chase was at the office, and since Kristina had sounded very insistent that Odelia come over immediately, she felt she better do as she asked and hadn't informed her husband.

"It could be a trap," Dooley said in the car on the drive over. "The Careens killed that insurance man and now they're going to kill every single witness to their crime!"

"I very much doubt that that's the case, Dooley," I said.

"But she's pregnant, Max! We have to protect her lump!"

"And we will protect her bump. We're right here for her, aren't we?"

My friend was only slightly mollified by this, seeing as two cats don't exactly an army make. Then again, we couldn't very well ask Chase to accompany us everywhere we went, now could we? The man had other things to do as well, and being his wife's bodyguard was going to become a full-time job if it was up to Dooley.

We arrived there posthaste, and Kristina opened the door even before Odelia applied index finger to doorbell. "You have to see this," she said, and hurried into her cozy little home, then proceeded to hand Odelia a little black book, turned to a specific page. The little black book looked like it had been through the wars, but it was still readable enough.

Odelia sat down on a chair and studied the page indicated with a frown. "This looks like something a garage owner wrote," she said finally. "Pieces ordered, work done on cars, prices worked out…"

"Look here," said Kristina, and stabbed a finger to the page heading.

"October 14," Odelia read, then looked up with a puzzled expression.

"Poppy was killed October 13," said Kristina.

Odelia slowly took in the rest of the page. "Green Mustang. New front bumper and grille," she read. "Dent repair and paintwork right front fender."

"It's the car that killed Poppy," said Kristina. "I'm sure it is. Look at the first page."

Odelia turned to the first page. "Jefferson Gusta. Gusta Garage," she read.

"Don't you see? The person who hit my little girl had their car fixed first thing. New bumper, new fender, body-work, paint job. And all off the books." She tapped the little black book. "Gusta Garage must have done this kind of off-the-books jobs all the time. This is for one month only, so he must have kept a separate account for the money he received under the table. And the car that was used to kill Poppy was one of them."

"How did you get a hold of this?" asked Odelia.

"It came in the post this morning," said Kristina, and showed Odelia the envelope it had arrived in.

"There's no stamp," said Odelia. "Which means the person who delivered this must be connected to the Gusta Garage."

"Oh…" said Kristina, taken aback. "I thought the mailman…" She looked up and stared in the direction of the hallway. "So whoever delivered this…"

"Is someone who wishes you well," said Odelia, tapping the little note that had been in the envelope along with the notebook.

"There's a license plate in there," said Kristina. She'd taken the book and leafed to the page of significance. "Here," she said, holding out the book. "See? This is the car that hit Poppy and Rick that night. This is the evidence we need—the evidence the police have been looking for!"

Odelia placed the notebook on the table. "Can I take this?"

"Of course." She gave Odelia a gratified smile. "This is it, isn't it? This is the missing link."

"It might very well be," Odelia agreed, though she didn't sound as excited as Kristina. "I'm going to give this to my husband," she announced. "And he'll run a check on this Jefferson Gusta, and check the license plate. If this is what you think it is, we might be able to finally identify the man who killed your daughter, Kristina."

Kristina laughed. "Oh, God. Finally!"

"I wonder who delivered this to you," said Odelia. She'd taken a small plastic bag from her purse and now slipped the notebook inside. It looked like the kind of baggie people use to clean up after their dog did doodoo, but I knew better. It was an evidence bag.

"I wonder who this well-wisher is," said Kristina. "And why they waited thirteen years."

"It looks charred," said Odelia, studying the notebook through the plastic. "As if someone tried to burn it." Then she gave Kristina a reassuring smile. "You did well to call me."

Kristina quirked a quizzical eyebrow. "You mean, instead of asking my husband and son to go out and murder Jefferson Gusta?"

"You know that's not what I mean."

"Yesterday you seemed pretty sure that my boys are responsible for Morro's murder."

"We have to track down every lead, Kristina."

"I know." She'd clasped her hands together. "You'll keep me informed, won't you?"

"Of course I will."

The two women shared a warm hug, and then we took our leave.

The moment we were in the car, Odelia was already on the phone with her husband, relating the story to him, and giving him that license plate number to check. Moments later, he came back with a name.

"Dunc Hanover," she said, glancing in our direction. "Well, we better have a chat with Mr. Hanover."

CHAPTER 13

Harriet glanced around. She had to confess she was a little nervous. She'd never been on an undercover assignment like this before, and she didn't want to screw it up.

"It'll be fine," Brutus said as he gave her a reassuring smile.

"I hope so," said Harriet. "I don't want to disappoint Max."

It was Max who'd given them this assignment, when he'd suggested to Odelia last night that someone needed to go in and keep an eye on Omar Wissinski. It had come to the big orange cat's attention that following the murder of Omar's business partner Jona Morro, their secretary had quit her job on the spot. Apparently she didn't feel comfortable working in a place where such a gruesome murder had been committed.

Odelia had made the suggestion that Gran step in and apply for the vacancy, but the latter thought it was probably a better idea if Scarlett step up to the plate and did the honors. Scarlett had a way with the male contingent, after all, and wouldn't have a problem wrapping Omar around her little finger. Or another part of her anatomy.

And Gran was right: the moment Scarlett had walked into the office and offered her secretarial services, Omar had hired her on the spot. Because he'd obviously been in a spot. Not many people, it turns out, want to work for a man whose business partner has recently been murdered in a holdup.

And so there they now sat: Scarlett behind her desk, with strict instructions to assure anyone who called or dropped by that Morro & Wissinski was open for business, and Harriet and Brutus ensconced under the desk, taking it all in.

Scarlett had introduced them as her support animals, and Omar had simply waved an impatient hand and said, "Fine, fine. As long as you can start right now it's all fine!"

And start right now Scarlett most certainly had!

"I just wish that we were in the same room," Scarlett said as she stared at the closed door of her new employer's inner office. "I mean, how am I supposed to spy on the man when I can't even see him?"

"You could always try listening at the door," Harriet suggested, but of course Scarlett couldn't understand a word she said. It was the one thing that hampered this particular assignment, but that couldn't be helped.

"Just show her," Brutus suggested.

"Good idea, sweetie," said Harriet, and sashayed over to the door of the big boss's office and ostensively placed her ear against it. Scarlett watched on, and immediately caught her drift, for she came tripping over on her high heels and followed Harriet's example.

"I just hope he won't catch us!" she whispered.

"You just have to be quick!" Harriet whispered back.

Inside, Omar was in conference with his mother, who'd dropped by to check on her son, and presumably make sure he didn't have a car suspended above his desk as well.

"All you have to do is apologize to your dad," said Julia Wissinski. "And I'm sure he'll do the right thing!"

"Me apologize to him? It's him that needs to apologize to me, Mom!"

"Oh, don't be so stubborn, Omar. You know what your father is like."

"Look, I did nothing wrong, so I really don't see why I should go and grovel."

"It's not groveling! It's simply being smart."

"No," said Omar. "I'm not doing it."

"But, son!"

"I said no! I'm the oldest—not Argyle. So I really don't see why—"

"Oh, you're hopeless. Just like your father. You two really are cut from the same cloth, aren't you? Both as stubborn as mules!"

There was a sound of shuffling feet inside, and Harriet quickly nudged Scarlett, and they both hurried back to the desk. And just in time, too, for Scarlett had only just taken a seat, when the door to the inner office swung open and Julia Wissinski appeared, with her son right behind her, his face red and clearly in the throes of some powerful emotion.

"Please reconsider, Omar," said Mrs. Wissinski.

"No means no, Mom," said Omar, not to be dissuaded.

"Ooh!" his mother cried, throwing up her hands in obvious frustration, then stalked off, without deigning Scarlett even a single glance.

Omar stood there, silently fuming for a few moments, his jaw working furiously as he did, then he cut a fiery look to Scarlett. "Any calls for me?"

"No, Mr. Wissinski, sir," said Scarlett meekly. "No one has called."

"Hrmph," said Omar, then retreated into his inner sanctum, and slammed the door.

"What was that all about?" asked Harriet.

"No idea," said Brutus, "but we better tell Max. Maybe he'll be able to figure it out."

"Don't think we need to," said Harriet, and gestured to Scarlett, who'd picked up her phone and was dialing a number.

Gran's friend had lowered her voice, and whispered into her phone, "Omar's mom was here, Vesta. She and Omar had a big fight. No, I don't know what it was about. Something about him having to apologize to his dad, and refusing to. Yeah, big blowup, apparently."

Just then, the door to the outer office swung open and an elderly lady walked in, glanced around for a moment to get her bearings, then made a beeline for Scarlett.

"Gotta go!" Scarlett whispered, and hung up.

"I want to see Mr. Wissinski," the old lady demanded.

"I'll see if he's available," said Scarlett in honeyed tones. "Who can I say is calling?"

"Leta Stooge," said the woman, enunciating clearly. "My son Gene was in here yesterday, but apparently one of the partners had just been murdered." She arched an eyebrow, as if she didn't approve of this kind of outlandish behavior on the part of her insurance agent. "I hope Mr. Wissinski hasn't been murdered, too?"

"No, Mr. Wissinski is fine."

"Good. I don't mind if he's murdered, but not before he gives me back my money."

Scarlett picked up the phone and moments later was in a brief conference with her employer. And even though Omar had only recently inquired if new customers had paid a visit to their offices, clearly he wasn't as eager as he could have been to see Mrs. Stooge.

"He'll be with you shortly," said Scarlett, as she gestured

to the waiting area and offered Mrs. Stooge a cup of coffee or tea while she waited.

The woman didn't seem predisposed either to waiting or to cups of tea or coffee, but she decided to do as she was told, and took a seat next to a potted plant, then picked up a copy of *Insurers Weekly* from the table in the waiting area and started leafing through it.

Finally Omar managed to screw up his nerve and the door to his office opened once more. "Mrs. Stooge? I can see you now, if you please."

The older lady, head held high, stalked past the man and straight into his office.

"Please hold my calls, Miss Canyon," said Omar, looking a little feverish all of a sudden.

"Let's go!" Harriet said, and hurried over to the man's door, Scarlett and Brutus right behind her.

"I know my son came in here yesterday," they heard Mrs. Stooge declare, "and I know you gave him some kind of runaround. You won't do the same with me, Mr. Wissinski. I want my money back and I want it now!"

"See, the problem is that we were robbed, Mrs. Stooge," said Omar. "And I explained all this to Gene yesterday. Our safe was emptied out, as in everything was taken."

"But surely you have money in your account?"

"I'm afraid we hadn't yet transferred the money you gave me to the bank."

"So my money was in your safe?"

"Yes, it was. And it's all gone now."

"But aren't you insured against this sort of thing? I mean, you are an insurance agent, aren't you? Insuring stuff is what you do."

They heard Omar heave a loud sigh. "The problem is, Mrs. Stooge, and I'm very sorry to have to inform you of this, that it now looks as if my partner was engaged in activities that weren't exactly above board."

"You mean he was cheating?"

"We're still trying to figure out what Jona was up to, but as far as I can figure out, he used the money that you and some other people invested in our bitcoin fund to finance his own extracurricular activities. In other words, all the money that was received was received off the books."

"Under the table."

"So it would seem."

"And you're telling me you weren't aware of this?"

"No, I wasn't. It's only after what happened yesterday that I discovered certain irregularities in the accounts. You see, Jona was in charge of our investments while I took care of the insurance policies."

"But you sold me on your bitcoin fund! Said I was going to triple my investment!"

"That was Jona's project, too. I was just the middleman. The salesperson, if you will."

"Well, I'll be damned."

"I'm very sorry, Mrs. Stooge. But with the robbery, all this has now come to light, and a very thorough investigation is being carried out. I've requested an extensive audit of our books, and hopefully we'll get to the bottom of this mess very quickly."

"So Jona was a crook, was he?"

"I wouldn't go so far as to—"

"Well, I will. The man was a thief!"

"The investigation will have to bear that out."

"Do you think that's why he was killed? For getting involved with the wrong people?"

"It's possible. I have no idea what he used the money for, but I have heard rumors that Jona had a gambling problem and may have had trouble paying back some of the people he borrowed money from. Now the police have been informed, and so it's only a matter of time before the people who did this to him are caught."

"Hopefully they haven't spent my money yet," Mrs. Stooge grumbled.

"We'll just have to wait and see, I'm afraid."

"Well, this is a fine mess you put me in, young man."

"And I'm very, very sorry, Mrs. Stooge. This is not the way to treat a loyal and treasured client like yourself, but if you give me some time, I hope to get this all sorted out soon."

"Fine," said Mrs. Stooge, and Harriet heard the telltale sound of a chair being scraped back.

"Move out!" she loud-whispered, and she and her co-conspirators quickly resumed their position at Scarlett's desk.

They were getting the hang of this, since moments later the door to Omar's office opened, and Mrs. Stooge came charging through the office, like a galleon under steam.

"If she comes back," said Omar, who looked a little soluble after his conference with the irate older lady, "tell her I'm out, will you?" He let out a long sigh. "A couple more of these and I'm going to wish someone dropped a car on top of my head, too."

And he would probably have said more, but his phone chimed and he picked it out of his pocket, glanced at the screen, then picked up with a grunted, "What do you want?!" He listened for a moment, then his eyes went a little wide and he clasped at his hair. "What?! Have you gone completely mad!" He disconnected, charged into his office, grabbed his coat, and charged past Scarlett's desk. "Mind the shop. I'll be back in half an hour."

And without further explanation, he was gone.

"Phew," said Scarlett, sagging a little in her chair. "Now

isn't this fun?" She picked up her own phone, and said, "He's gone, Vesta. Yeah, the coast is clear!"

Moments later there was a knock at the door, and since it was a glass door, Harriet could see that it was Gran. The old lady came in looking excited, and immediately took a seat in front of Scarlett's desk. "And? What did you find out so far?"

"A lot!" said Scarlett, equally excited. "Omar is having a fight with his dad over something, and a Mrs. Stooge came in here, and Omar revealed to her that Jona was actually a secret gambler and owed a lot of money to the wrong people. Which might explain why he was murdered!"

Gran narrowed her eyes. "So you think his murder had nothing to do with the Careens?"

"Well, it's possible, isn't it? Apparently Jona was collecting money from pensioners to invest in his bitcoin fund, but it was all kept off the books. Cash payments only, and the money kept in the safe."

"Which was emptied out yesterday. It's possible, of course. Those loan sharks don't mess around. If you don't pay up, you will pay the price."

"But why kill him?" asked Harriet. "Wouldn't they want Jona alive, so he can pay back his loan?"

"Sometimes these people like to set an example," said Gran. "So they kill someone in such a gruesome way that it sends a message to anyone else who owes them money: better pay up quick, or end up like this guy."

"It's a plausible theory," said Scarlett, nodding. "So where did you set up shop?"

"In the food court," said Gran. "It's nice and cozy there, and I'm surrounded by plenty of people my age, so I don't stick out. And the best thing: they don't pressure you into leaving if you're not prepared to drink your body weight in coffee."

"Good. I'll join you there for lunch," said Scarlett, "and I'll tell you everything!"

"Ooh, there's more?"

"By the time my lunch break rolls around, I definitely hope so!"

Harriet shared a smile with Brutus. Clearly the two ladies were having a ball. Max was right. This job was right up their alley. And it was right up hers and Brutus's, too.

"I like this spy business," her mate intimated.

"Yeah, me too," said Harriet.

"So have you given any more thought to the bitcoin thing?"

"I have, but we're going to need a programmer to set up the website." And they both looked up to Scarlett, whose grandnephew was some kind of computer whizz.

"What?" asked Gran, who caught her cats' look.

"We need Kevin to set up a bitcoin website for us," said Harriet. "So we can start collecting money for HarrietCoin."

"Or BrutusCoin," Brutus piped up.

"What is it?" asked Scarlett.

"Harriet wants Kevin to set up a website for her new bitcoin."

"Bitcoin! But isn't that some kind of scam?"

"It's not a scam!" Harriet cried, not for the first time.

"I think it's a scam," said Gran determinedly. "And frankly that kind of thing is behind me now, Harriet."

"What do you mean?" asked Harriet, eyes wide.

"The scammy stuff! I'm going to be a great-grandma soon. I can't afford to go to jail for fleecing pensioners. I mean, you heard what Scarlett said. The kind of thing you're suggesting is exactly what Jona Morro was into. And look how that turned out."

"But Gran!"

"No means no, Harriet. I don't want to get murdered by

car before I have a chance to hold my great-grandkid in my arms. So the life of crime is a thing of the past for me."

"But it's not a scam, Gran! It's all above board."

"Tell that to Leta Stooge." She wagged a finger in Harriet's face. "And you better get wise, too, missy. Or you'll end up in the pound!"

Harriet gulped, and so did Brutus. "Not the pound!" Brutus cried.

And there ended Harriet's dream of becoming outrageously rich by selling bitcoin to unsuspecting people. It worked for Elon Musk, but clearly it wasn't gonna work for her.

Oh, hell and damnation!

CHAPTER 14

Dunc Hanover was hard at work in his atelier. His main claim to fame were his life-sized papier-mâché figures. They were colorful, lifelike, and had brought him all over the world, in museums and exhibitions from New York to Paris or even Lisbon, Portugal, where they had a particular predilection for his remarkable and original work.

His atelier, basically an old glue factory that had been turned into lofts, was located on the outskirts of town, and it was where he was always happiest. He could have worked from home, of course, but ever since he'd become engaged, his future wife preferred if he kept their home life and his professional life separate.

And he didn't blame her. Like a lot of artists, he had a tendency to get a little obsessed when he was working, and forget not only about his surroundings but even himself: he forgot to eat, take a bath, get dressed. He could easily go for days with only the bare minimum of personal care, and that wasn't the kind of thing a loving partner enjoyed.

So when he was working on his next project, he liked to do it here, and make sure Justina didn't have to fret when he waltzed through the living room looking like a scarecrow. She knew that he always came out of these periods of frenzied creativity, and when he did, he was like any regular Joe. It was the life they'd made for themselves, and they were both more than happy with it, even though other couples might not be.

He stood back and inspected the latest model he'd been working on. It didn't quite look the way he imagined it yet. The chicken-wire framework was there, and now he had to start draping large pieces of papier-mâché onto that, before letting those dry, and then the next part could begin: applying his trademark bright coloring. And when that was done, a final thick layer of varnish added the finishing touch.

A noise had him look up in surprise. When he glanced over, and saw who his visitor was, he frowned. He didn't like to be disturbed when he was working. It took him out of his creative flow. "What are you doing here?" he grumbled, his eye having turned back to size up the next challenge. And then he had it: the frame was too big. Too large. Of course. And he probably would have set about to fix the proportions if not a heavy object had come crashing down on the back of his skull.

Moments later he was spread out on the floor.

CHAPTER 15

Odelia had picked up her husband in town, and together we made our way to the atelier where according to his fiancée we would be able to find Dunc Hanover, the well-known artist. I'm saying well-known even though I'd never heard of him. But since he had a Wikipedia page, and on this Wikipedia page it said he was famous, I guess it must be true, since Wikipedia never lies, does it?

"So let me get this straight," said Chase, who was riding shotgun for once. "It wasn't Jona Morro who drove the car that fateful night, but Dunc Hanover?"

"According to the notebook that Jefferson Gusta kept it was Hanover," said Odelia.

"And Gusta fixed up the car the next morning, and got rid of any evidence that Hanover had been involved in a hit and run with deadly consequences."

"What I don't get is how this notebook suddenly turned up thirteen years after the fact, and who hand-delivered it to Kristina."

"We better have a little chat with Gusta later."

"Gran also called."

Chase smiled. "Reporting from her undercover mission, is she?"

"Yeah, turns out that Jona Morro was the one behind the bitcoin business. He'd told Omar to collect money from his clients to invest in their bitcoin fund, but to keep everything off the books. Omar thinks he needed the money to pay back a gambling debt. He claims that his business partner owed money to the wrong people, and that's why he was killed yesterday."

"We better look into that as well. So that would mean that Morro's death isn't connected to the Careens."

"According to Omar Wissinski, at least."

"Pity Morro isn't around anymore to confirm or deny."

We'd arrived at the old factory building that had been turned into fancy lofts, and Odelia parked in front of the building. "Nicely done," she said as we approached.

And they had indeed done a great job. They'd kept the red brick, but had completely remodeled the building, and added all the modern conveniences your homeowner likes, like a video intercom and a state-of-the-art elevator. It all looked very expensive.

"I wonder how much these lofts go for," said Chase as we waited for Mr. Hanover to buzz us in.

"Why? Are you in the market for a loft?" asked Odelia.

Chase shrugged. "Just curious." He frowned when no response came, and pressed the bell once more. "Looks like our Mr. Hanover isn't home," he finally announced. He pressed more bells, and finally someone buzzed us in, probably just to get rid of the noise.

We entered and the elevator soon whisked us up to the top floor, where the artist had taken up residence.

When we arrived, the steel door was ajar, and so we pushed our way inside. It was a spacious loft. In fact it looked as if it comprised the entire floor, which was enormous.

"Hello!" Chase called out, and his voice echoed in the vast space. Above us, slanted windows offered a view of a blue sky, and around us, large sculptures testified to the presence of the artist.

"They're papier-mâché," Odelia explained as we studied one. The work of art was bigger than Chase, and was very colorful. It also shone as if it had been freshly varnished. "It's Dunc Hanover's claim to fame. I once interviewed him, and he's very proud of his work. Says it's his ambition to create at least a thousand of these figures in his lifetime."

There were dozens of them spread around the atelier, like sentinels standing guard. They reminded me of that army a Chinese emperor was once buried with, though they had been made of terracotta, and not papier-mâché, of course.

We ventured further into the artist's space, and soon came upon what looked like a brand-new installation. Several half-finished figures stood at attention, and a few that were only in their initial stages and consisted of what looked like chicken wire sculpted into the shape of a human. As I understood, this was the framework the paper was to be draped on.

And then I saw it: one of those chicken-wire figures was half-finished, with pieces of wet paper stuck to them. Only when I looked at the head, it looked very lifelike indeed. Too lifelike, in fact. For inside the frame, a real person was standing... and he looked very much dead to me!

"Odelia!" I cried, pointing to the figure.

"Oh, my God!" she said, and she and Chase quickly hurried over. But when Chase felt the man's pulse by pressing his fingers into his neck, he shook his head.

"He's gone," he said as he stepped back.

. . .

69

Fifteen minutes later, the place was buzzing with activity. Abe Cornwall had arrived with his team, and they were dusting the area for prints, looking for DNA evidence, and checking the body.

"Well, he's dead, all right," said Abe finally. He removed his plastic gloves.

"How did he die?" asked Odelia.

"Too soon to tell. First we have to get him out of that... thing." He frowned. "What is it?"

"One of his papier-mâché figures," said Odelia. "He was famous for them."

"Looks like the killer has a warped sense of humor," said Abe. "He seems to have wanted to turn the artist into one of his works of art."

Just then, a loud voice called out, "Oh, my God! What's happened!"

We all turned, and found ourselves looking into the familiar face of Omar Wissinski.

"What are you doing here, Mr. Wissinski?" asked Chase, none too friendly.

"I just got a call from Dunc," said Wissinski. "He said he was getting married!"

Chase and Odelia took the insurance broker aside, out of sight of his friend's dead body. He looked very much stricken, and it wouldn't surprise me if he hadn't yet fully recovered from that thump on the head he'd received the day before.

"Dead?" asked Omar. "But I-I don't understand."

"We think he was killed," said Chase, never afraid to be the bearer of bad news.

"Killed! But why? And by who?"

"We don't know yet. So tell me, why are you here?"

"I told you. Dunc said he was getting married."

"So you came to congratulate him? Suggest to be his best man? What?"

"No, of course not! I came here to stop him!"

Now we all stared at the man.

"He's a little nutty, isn't he, Max?" said Dooley.

"I'm not sure, Dooley," I said. "Maybe there's a method to his madness."

"Look, I'm Dunc's buddy," Omar explained.

"Yes, I know. You were good friends with Dunc Hanover."

Omar shook his head irritably. "Not just friends. I was also Dunc's buddy."

"You mean like in the AA?" asked Chase.

"Yeah, exactly like the AA. That's where we got the idea. You see, we're confirmed bachelors, all of us, and the buddy system was supposed to make sure we all stayed that way. So of course when Dunc told me he was getting married, I had to see him."

"To talk him out of it?" asked Odelia.

"Yes, of course! It's what a buddy does. I wouldn't be much of a friend if I'd simply let him go through with it, now would I?"

"But… marriage isn't an addiction, is it?"

Omar gave her the kind of look one gives a layperson. A person who just doesn't get it. "Look, we all swore a solemn oath many years ago, that none of us would ever get ensnared by a woman—or a man, for that matter. And we took our oath very seriously. We like the bachelor life," he said, spreading his arms. "It's the only life for any sane person. And I was Dunc's buddy the same way that he was mine."

"Who else is in that group?" asked Chase.

"Well, Jona," said Omar, "and Sergio Sorbet and Joel Timperley."

Chase and Odelia shared a look. It was those five joyriders again. The ones the Careens accused of having killed Poppy and then closing ranks to hide the identity of her killer.

"The five of you swore a solemn oath never to get married?" asked Odelia.

"Yes, we did. We were eighteen at the time, and even though we all had girlfriends, we hated the idea of being tied down. I have to add that for all of us, our parents didn't exactly set the example of what a happy relationship should look like. All of them were in a bad marriage, and so we decided that marriage was the last thing we wanted."

"And you stuck to your guns and never married."

"Until now, with Dunc." His face sort of crumpled. "And now he's dead!"

"Do you think his death has got anything to do with this bachelor's pledge?"

Omar frowned and fingered his corrugated brow. "I-I don't know." He looked up. "You think it might? But how?"

"One of your merry bachelors, perhaps?"

"Are you crazy? Of course not. Dunc is one of my best friends."

"Where were you just now, sir?" asked Chase.

"I was at the office. You can ask my new secretary. Miss Canyon. She'll confirm it." He was staring at Chase, as if horrified by the notion that he'd ever hurt his friend—and bachelor buddy.

"He looks very disappointed that his buddy is dead, Max," said Dooley.

"Yeah, now he doesn't have anyone to keep him from getting married," I said.

"Is marriage such a bad thing?"

"It depends if you're in a good marriage or a bad one, I guess."

"Chase and Odelia are in a good marriage, though, right?"

"Oh, yes, a very good one. And so are Marge and Tex."

"And Brutus and Harriet."

I smiled. "They're not married yet."

Dooley looked up at this. "Do you think they'll ever get married?"

"I doubt it. I've never heard of pets getting married."

"I have. Some dogs owned by people on Fifth Avenue in New York recently got married. They had a whole ceremony with an actual priest, and a big wedding feast for all their dog friends afterward. It was a big to-do."

"That's dogs, Dooley. Everyone knows that dogs are weird."

"True," he agreed. "Dogs and humans both."

CHAPTER 16

Justina McMenamy was a beautiful woman, and if her fiancé Dunc Hanover had lived, would have made a gorgeous bride. As it was, their marriage wasn't to be, and after Justina had cried bitter tears of shock and surprise, she turned angry, and lashed out at her fiancé's 'so-called friends' who surely were to blame for the man's death.

"They did it," she said as she spoke to Chase and Odelia, seated at her kitchen table in her cozy little home. "They're the ones you should talk to."

"His bachelor friends?" asked Odelia.

"Of course! They swore a stupid oath that they would never get married, and clearly the oath also assumed that they would do whatever it took to prevent any one of them from getting married—including murder!"

"So you think Wissinski, Sorbet or Timperley killed your fiancé?" asked Chase.

"Absolutely." She sighed and seemed to sag. "Dunc wasn't like them, you see. They were all trust fund kids. Rich spoiled brats. But Dunc wasn't. His parents weren't rich like the others. His mom was a seamstress and his dad worked for Amtrak. But somehow he'd become friends with them, and even though he wasn't in the same social class, they accepted him, and invited him to hang out. They even paid for him to be included in school trips that his parents couldn't possibly afford. And even after they left school, they all remained friends. But by then Dunc had discovered his passion for art, and decided that he wanted to become an artist. And they backed him, against his parents' wishes."

"He was a great artist," said Odelia. "We saw his work at his atelier."

"He was a genius," said Justina. "An absolute genius. And he made it all on his own. He became famous and wealthy through his art, not because of an inheritance or his parents' trust fund, which made him all the more heroic in my opinion."

"But why would his friends want to murder him?" asked Chase. "That doesn't make any sense."

"It does to them. They have this warped idea that marriage is evil, and that it must be prevented at all cost. Which is why Dunc didn't want anyone to know that we were together. He never wanted to be seen with me, and never mentioned me to his friends."

"You were his guilty secret?"

"Yes, I was. At least to those four idiots. They wouldn't have accepted it if Dunc had come right out and admitted that he'd fallen in love and wanted to get married."

"But he must have told them at some point—he told Omar Wissinski this morning."

"Omar was the one he was closest to. So it stands to reason he'd tell him."

"Do you think he told the others, too?"

Justina nodded. "He must have. And you see what

happened. He told them and now he's dead. Draw your own conclusion. I know I have." She broke into a fresh wave of tears, with Odelia handing her a tissue to stem the flood. "He was such a sweet man. So tender. Not like the others." She shook her head. "I never understood how he could be friends with them. They were so different. So very different."

"Did Dunc ever mention an incident that took place thirteen years ago?" asked Odelia. "A hit-and-run accident where a little girl was killed?"

Justina frowned. "I don't think so. I think I'd remember if he did."

"We have reason to believe that it was his car that was involved. The day after the accident a green Mustang was brought into a garage and the mechanic was asked to make sure that all traces of the accident were removed. The mechanic kept a notebook, recording every job he did, right down to license plates and the work involved. Which is how we know that it was your fiancé's car that killed Poppy Careen that night."

"He never mentioned any of that to me."

"What do you think happened to that Mustang?" asked Chase.

"Dunc doesn't even own a car. He got rid of it years ago, and has refused to drive one ever since."

"Did he tell you why?"

"He hated cars. Said they are the cause of too much pain and suffering."

Chase and Odelia shared a look. "That could be why he got rid of it," said Odelia. "Because of the accident. He refused to drive a car ever again after what happened."

"It's possible," Justina allowed. "But like I said, he never mentioned an accident to me."

"Thank you for your time, Miss McMenamy," said Chase, getting up.

"Talk to his friends, will you?" said Justina. "Find out which one of them killed Dunc." Her voice broke. "And make them pay. Make them all pay!"

CHAPTER 17

"Odd," said Dooley once we were in the car again.

"What is?" I asked.

"Well, he was an artist, and now he's been turned into a work of art himself."

"Yeah, as if the killer was trying to make a point. But what point? And why?"

"Do you think his friends killed him because he wanted to get married?"

"It's possible, of course," I said. "But it seems like a very weak motive to want to kill a person, don't you think?"

"Unless you really, really hate marriage."

"Yeah, I guess." I thought about Justina's words. She really seemed convinced that one of Dunc's friends was behind his murder, so at the very least we had to talk to them. But still, it all seemed like a strange coincidence that first Jona Morro would be killed, and now Dunc. And Jona's murder seemed connected to his gambling habit, while Dunc... "Do you think Dunc was a gambler?" I asked, addressing Odelia.

She half-turned to me. "You mean, because of his connection to Jona Morro?"

"It would explain why both friends died in similar circumstances only a day apart."

"Would you say the circumstances of both deaths are similar? Morro was killed in a holdup, and as far as we can make out, nothing was taken from Dunc Hanover's loft."

"Yeah, you're right," I said, sinking back onto the backseat once more.

"What is he saying?" asked Chase.

"He's looking for a connection between Jona Morro's murder and Dunc Hanover's."

"The only connection I see is that they were friends and were both involved in the hit-and-run accident that killed Poppy Careen."

"So we're back to that, are we?" asked Odelia.

Chase nodded. "We better find out if Dominic and Rick Careen have an alibi for this morning. And can you ask Scarlett when exactly Wissinski left his office?"

"Do you think he could have killed his friend?"

"You heard what Justina said. These guys seem to take this bachelor business pretty seriously."

"If that's what killed Dunc, we better talk to the other two bachelors. Joel Timperley and Sergio Sorbet."

"Zeus!" Chase grunted.

"You're a fan, aren't you?"

"Oh, yeah."

"Well, you'll get to meet him soon."

"We're going to meet Zeus, Max?" asked Dooley.

"We're going to meet the actor who plays Zeus," I clarified. "Not the real Zeus."

"Is there a real Zeus? And does he control the weather?"

"I doubt it, Dooley. At least I've never seen him, have you?"

"Al Roker?"

"He doesn't make the weather, he just presents it."

"Oh, right."

Once more we paid a visit to Dominic and his son in the woods. They were still as reluctant to give us the time of day as before, and claimed they hadn't left their precious woods all morning, and had definitely not snuck away to go and kill Dunc Hanover. It all sounded very convenient, with father and son providing each other with an alibi.

As far as I was concerned, their involvement seemed a lot more plausible than the bachelor murder theory Justina had put forward as a possible motive. But as long as we couldn't place Dominic or Rick at the scene of the crime, there was nothing we could do.

"Maybe Dominic and Rick are going through the list of bachelors one by one," said Dooley once we were en route to the Keystone Mall to have a chat with the mall's owner Joel Timperley. "Maybe they're going to kill all of them, just to make sure that the person who killed Poppy is dead. So maybe we should have told them that it was actually Dunc who drove the car that night. Otherwise they'll keep on killing these men."

"It's an interesting theory," I said. "And it sure looks as if the Careens have something to hide. But I'm not sure if they'd suddenly turn into mass murderers thirteen years after Poppy was killed."

"But Kristina is sick, Max. In fact she's dying. And I think her husband and son want to make sure that before she dies, the men who killed Poppy are all punished."

"It's possible," I allowed. "But if it's true, it's impossible to prove right now."

"Well, we better prove it fast, or else we'll soon run out of bachelors."

. . .

We were in Joel Timperley's office, which was located on the top floor of the mall, and offered a great view of its surrounding area. Mostly fields, as far as I could tell, and one sprawling housing development. There were in fact a lot of different businesses who'd set up shop at the mall, and Timperley was only one of them, though probably the most important one, since they owned the entire mall, and many more like it.

"So what can I do for you?" asked Mr. Timperley. His office was big, and right in the center of it, a model of his family's mall had been placed, though it looked a little different from the actual mall. Joel noticed that Chase was studying the model, and he got up from behind his desk with athletic alacrity and joined us. "We're expanding," he explained.

"Business going well?" asked Chase.

"So well we need additional space."

"I've heard that a lot of malls are actually closing. Competition with online stores."

"Then I guess we're the odd ones out. And Keystone Mall is still the best one out of the hundred or so we're now operating all across the country. Though of course Keystone holds a special place in our hearts, since it was the first mall my family built. Keystone was the key to our success, you might say." He grinned, showing perfect white teeth.

Joel Timperley was a handsome young man, and looked as if he spent as much time in the gym as the boardroom. He was dressed to impress in an expensive suit that still managed to look fashionable, and had the cockiness of a successful young entrepreneur.

"I'm afraid we have some bad news for you, sir," said Chase, finally getting to the heart of our reason for being there. "Your friend Dunc Hanover... has just been found dead."

Joel's jaw sagged. "Dunc? Dead? But how?"

"He was murdered."

"Murdered!"

"I'm afraid so, sir. We found him in his atelier, the victim of foul play."

"Did you know that Dunc was engaged to be married, sir?" asked Odelia.

Joel had sunk down on his swivel chair and looked distressed. "Um… yeah. Yeah, he told me last month. Said he met a very special woman, and had proposed."

"And how did that make you feel, sir?" asked Chase.

"I was surprised, of course. But happy for him. Dunc is a great guy—was." He stared down at his desk, still coming to terms with the tragedy that had befallen his friend.

"So you weren't upset about it? Angry that he would break the bachelor oath?"

"What?" Joel looked up with a frown. "What do you mean?"

"We talked to Omar Wissinski," said Chase. "And he told us that he was Dunc's buddy. That his task was to keep his friend on the straight and narrow. In this case in a state of bachelorhood. He was very shocked when Dunc told him he was going to get married."

"Yeah, I know. Omar was the last person he told. And that's because Omar took the whole bachelor business more seriously than the rest of us. You see, Omar's parents had a pretty lousy marriage, and it made Omar take a dim view on the married state."

"We also talked to Dunc's fiancée Justina McMenamy," said Odelia. "And she told us she believes that one of Dunc's friends is responsible for his murder. Once again because he had chosen not to remain a bachelor."

Joel rocked up from his chair. "But that's ridiculous! Dunc

was one of my best friends! He even asked me to be his best man!"

"You were going to be his best man?"

"Absolutely! And proud to be. I loved Dunc like a brother —always have. Now why in the world would I want to hurt him?"

"Where were you between eleven and twelve this morning, sir?" asked Chase.

"Right here," said Joel, sitting down again. "Just ask my secretary. I'm always here—always working."

"This is where all of your malls and supermarkets are managed from?" asked Odelia.

"That's right. The entire Timperley business empire, if you can call it that, is managed from this office. Like my dad managed it before me, and my grandfather before him."

"There's one other matter we need to discuss," said Chase.

"What?" asked Joel, his exuberance having taken a serious hit.

"You and your friends were out joyriding thirteen years ago."

"Oh, God, not with the Poppy Careen business again!" said Joel, rubbing his face with his hands. "Look, we had nothing to do with that, all right? We were all interrogated over and over again, and nothing was ever proven. We weren't even there that night! We were in a completely different part of town."

"So why did Dunc Hanover spend the better part of the next morning having his car get a complete makeover to hide any traces of the accident he was in?"

Joel's jaw dropped at this, and he stared at Chase. "What are you talking about?"

"We have solid evidence that Dunc had his Mustang serviced on October 14th, the day after Poppy Careen was killed. More importantly, he had his front bumper replaced, and dents removed from the right side fender of the car and repainted. Why would he do that if not because he'd been in an accident the night before? The right side, not coincidentally, is the side that knocked her brother Rick off his bike."

"Look, it's possible that Dunc was in an accident that night, but he never went near that girl. None of us did."

"So you're saying he was involved in another accident, and the fact that he ordered a rush job to get his car fixed, and asked the mechanic to keep it off the books is just a coincidence? Or the fact that the damage corresponds with Poppy and Rick's injuries?"

Joel was nodding furiously. "Yes! Exactly! Look, we were a bunch of stupid kids back in the day, with too much time on our hands, and parents with too much money so we got to drive the kind of cars other kids could only dream of. So we spent a couple of weekends joyriding and doing all the kinds of stupid stuff kids do at that age. But we never killed anyone, or even injured anyone, for that matter. And the fact that Dunc had to bring his car into the garage the morning after one of those stupid stunts, well, that only proves that he must have hit some other car, or a tree or whatever. If you're going to drive through town at these crazy speeds and pull dangerous stunts, accidents will happen."

"So when we talk to the mechanic who worked on your friend's car, he will confirm that the damage to his car didn't come from hitting a little girl and her brother?"

"Of course!" But he didn't look entirely at ease. In fact he looked downright nervous now, and was sweating bullets.

"I think he's lying, Max," said Dooley.

"Yeah, I think so, too," I agreed.

Looks like we were on the right track.

CHAPTER 18

Scarlett's new boss looked licked when he returned to the office. He was pale and drawn and muttered something about not wanting to see any clients before retreating into his office and closing the door. But then of course they already knew what had happened to Dunc Hanover. Looks like Omar had arrived too late to save his friend.

"Maybe it was a good thing that he got there too late," said Harriet. "Or else he might now be dead, too, if he'd bumped into the murderer."

"Poor guy," said Brutus. "First one friend is killed and now another. If this keeps up he won't have any friends left."

"At least he still has his mother. They say a boy's best friend is his mother. Or is that a girl's best friend?"

The phone on Scarlett's desk chimed and she picked up. "Yes, sir?" she said.

"You better go home, Miss Canyon," said her boss. "Nothing more for you to do here."

"Thank you, sir. Will you be all right?"

"I'm fine," he said with a voice from the tomb. "Absolutely fine," and then he hung up.

"You heard the man," said Scarlett as she picked up her purse. "Let's go."

And so they left the office, their first day as undercover spies at an end. Harriet wasn't sure if they'd learned much of significance, but she was determined to give Max a full report. It was now his job to figure out if what they had to report would bring them closer to solving these murders or not.

We met up with Harriet and Brutus and Scarlett at the food court, which was pretty much the heart of the mall. It was also the place where most people were gathered. The tea room Gran had selected as her post was a popular one, but she didn't seem to mind all the activity, busy as she was with receiving Scarlett's regular updates on all things happening inside the offices of Morro & Wissinski.

"Oh, Max," said Harriet as she excitedly came tripping up. "Have we got news for you."

"Tell me all," I said as we took up position next to the table.

And so soon I learned all about the visit of Omar's mom, and of Mrs. Stooge, and the gambling habits of Omar's business partner, and of course the phone call Omar had received, presumably from Dunc to tell him he was about to get married, and also how dejected Omar had looked when he'd returned to the office just now. All in all, it was a good day's work for our undercover spies, and that's what I told Harriet and Brutus.

"I think this whole business must be connected to the Careens, don't you think, Max?" asked Harriet. "They're going to kill these bachelors one by one until there's no one left."

"That's exactly what I said!" said Dooley.

Harriet gave him a smile. "Great minds think alike, Dooley."

"And I think it's the gambling business that's key here," said Brutus. "Jona was an inveterate gambler, and probably Dunc was the same way. Only his girlfriend doesn't like to mention the fact, since he's a famous artist, and she doesn't want to ruin his reputation."

"You think so?" I asked, interested in Brutus's point of view.

"Of course! She wants to make sure that now that Dunc is dead, his work will still be sold, and if his reputation is destroyed, prices for his work might drop, and she doesn't want that."

"So you think the people who've been lending money to both Jona and Dunc have decided to start murdering all of the people that are in debt with them?" asked Harriet. "That just doesn't make any sense, darlington. For one thing, it's bad business to murder your clients, and for another: it draws too much attention."

"They're setting an example!"

"One example is fine, but two? That's overkill. And not necessary!"

"I think it's the Careens that are behind this," said Dooley.

"And I think it's the gamblers," said Brutus.

Suddenly they all turned to me. "So what do you think, Max?" said Brutus anxiously.

I shrugged. "Frankly I think it's too soon to tell. First we need to collect more information. More evidence. And then we'll be able to tell what happened exactly."

"And I'm afraid that if we wait much longer, more murders will be committed," said Harriet. "So you better think fast, Max!"

Oh, boy. Pressure. I hate pressure!

At the table where the humans sat, a similar conversation was taking place.

"Wanna know what I think?" said Gran.

"No, what?" said Odelia.

"I think Kristina Careen is behind these murders."

"Kristina Careen is agoraphobic, Gran. She doesn't leave the house."

"And I say that she does. This agoraphobia thing is just a front. When nobody's looking that woman sneaks out and goes and murders the people she thinks are responsible for her daughter's death."

"So you think she's faking it?" asked Scarlett.

"Of course she's faking it!"

"We talked to Kristina," said Chase. "And I don't think she's a fake, Vesta. She looked pretty genuine to me, and so does her illness."

"Are you a shrink? No, you're not. Talk to the shrink! He'll tell you I'm right."

"Kristina has a shrink?" asked Scarlett.

"Yeah, she's been in therapy for the past thirteen years," said Odelia.

"Then I don't think she's a fake, Vesta," said Scarlett. "Do you know how expensive these shrinks are? No one in their right mind would pay that much money and fake it."

"I'm not saying she's been faking it all these years. I'm saying that maybe in the past couple of weeks she discovered that she can leave the house and be fine. And instead of telling her family or her therapist she kept it a secret, so she can murder with absolute impunity." She shrugged. "I think Kristina Careen has mastered the perfect murder."

"The purr-fect murder," Harriet said with a grin. "How about that?"

"I doubt it, Gran," said Odelia. "You should have seen Kristina. She's not a fake."

"So who do you think is behind these murders? The bachelor brigade? Because one of them decided to get married? Are you going to tell me that Jona Morro was getting married, too?"

"We have no evidence of that," said Chase.

Scarlett sat up a little straighter. "Do you want me to ask Omar?"

"Do you think he'd tell you?" asked Gran.

"Oh, absolutely. That man is like an open book to me. He'll tell me anything I want to know. You should have seen him, the poor dear. Absolutely devastated." She rearranged her admittedly impressive décolletage. "So tomorrow morning, I'll offer him a nice cup of coffee and a shoulder to cry on."

"A shoulder, Scarlett," said Gran. "Not your... frontage."

Scarlett lightly slapped her friend's arm. "Vesta! Who do you take me for!"

"For a woman who'd do anything to extract information from her target," said Gran with a grin. "Just like me."

"Take it easy, Scarlett," said Odelia. "For all we know Omar could be behind these murders."

"But why? They were his best friends."

"Because they were both getting married?" Gran suggested.

"I doubt it. Omar is an absolute dear, and I'm going to prove it to you."

"When did he leave the office, exactly?" asked Chase.

"Um... around eleven?"

"We arrived at Dunc's loft at noon," said Chase. "And according to Abe the body was still warm, so the murder must have been committed shortly before we arrived."

"You could have caught the killer in action!" said Scarlett.

"Yeah, looks like we just missed him. When did Omar get there, babe?"

"Must have been around… twelve-fifteen? Something like that?"

"How long does it take to go from the mall to Gardner Street?"

"Ooh, let me!" said Scarlett, and took out her phone. "Google Maps," she said as she tapped her screen with her long fingernails.

"I don't know how she does it," said Harriet. "When I tap my tablet screen with my nails it doesn't work. I have to use my paw pads."

"I think it takes years of practice," I said as we all watched Scarlett with amusement.

"Got it!" she finally said, jiggling her 'frontage' for good measure. "Twenty minutes!"

"You have to take into consideration that he had to go from his office to the parking lot to get his car," said Gran. "So you better add another twenty minutes."

"Plus traffic and parking his car," Scarlett added. "Always a problem on Gardner Street."

"You know Gardner Street?" asked Odelia, surprised.

"My nail salon is in that building," said Scarlett, and held out her hands for Odelia's inspection.

"Nice," murmured the latter as she studied Scarlett's admittedly impressive nails.

"Okay, so that seems to pan out," said Chase. "I guess we can rule out Omar for Dunc's murder."

"And for Jona's murder as well," said Gran. "Unless the man would have knocked himself on the head."

"It's possible to knock yourself on the head," said Scarlett, and tried to demonstrate it, almost causing her to topple off her chair. "Okay, so maybe it's not that easy," she finally conceded. "Besides, like I said: Omar is a sweetie. He'd never raise his hand in anger."

"See?" said Gran triumphantly. "That only leaves Kristina —the fake agoraphobic!"

"Or her husband and son," said Odelia, giving her gran a censorious look.

"Or the gambling mafia," Chase grunted.

"Or one of the other bachelors!" said Scarlett. "Have you talked to Sergio yet?"

"Not yet," said Chase with a grin. "Why? You a fan of Zeus?"

Scarlett clutched a hand to her heart. "Am I a fan of Zeus? Are you kidding me! I'm only Zeus's biggest fan!" She wrapped a hand around Chase's impressive bicep. "Can I join you for the interview? I promise I won't do anything embarrassing like ask for the man's autograph." She batted her eyelids imploringly. "Pretty please?"

"This is a police investigation, Scarlett," said Chase, adopting his police persona and giving her a stern-faced look. "Not a press junket with a movie star."

"Oh, all right," she said, displaying a pouty face. "Be that way, if you must."

"We'll ask him for his autograph, if you want," Odelia suggested.

Scarlett perked up a little. "Have him make it out to 'My beloved Scarlett,' will you?"

Chase uttered a groan, but Odelia smiled and said, "I'll see what I can do."

CHAPTER 19

Since Odelia had retreated into her office and Chase had retreated into his, Dooley and I decided to pay a visit to our good friend Kingman and get his take on this whole murder business. Kingman is, after all, a bachelor, and maybe could offer us some unique perspective on the case.

"Two dead bachelors, huh?" he said as he lifted his head in greeting.

"One dead bachelor, actually," I said. "Dunc Hanover was engaged to be married."

"What can I tell you, fellas? It's always been the bachelor life for me."

"Technically we're also bachelors, aren't we, Max?" said Dooley. "I don't have a girlfriend and you don't have a girl-friend so I guess that also makes us bachelors."

"Yes, but not confirmed bachelors, like Kingman," I said, eager to make the distinction. "For Kingman being a bach-elor is like a vocation. Something he truly believes in."

"And for us?" Dooley asked. "What does being a bachelor mean for us, Max?"

"I guess… it just happens to be that way for us," I said.

"You mean like an accident?"

"Well, no. More like the way the cookie crumbles."

"What cookie?" he asked, his interest piqued.

"Any cookie, Dooley. It's just an expression."

"Chocolate chip, probably. I like chocolate, even though Vena says it's not good for me."

Vena is our vet, and has a long list of stuff that isn't good for us. Vena is a spoilsport.

We had met Kingman in front of the General Store, which is owned by his human Wilbur Vickery. Wilbur seemed to be in a bad mood for some reason, griping at his customers and generally looking grumpy and out of sorts.

"Max is right," said Kingman. "I am a bachelor out of conviction, whereas you guys are bachelors through no fault of your own—simply the fact that you haven't found the one yet."

"The one what?" asked Dooley.

"Well… the one," said Kingman with a helpless shrug. "Though in my personal opinion this whole business about the one is just a myth. I mean, why be so miserly, you know? Why can't there be two, or three, or even four or five 'ones' out there for everyone?"

Dooley seemed confused by all this talk of ones and two and threes. Then again, math has never been his strong suit, and neither has it been mine, I must confess.

Three fair felines came traipsing by at that moment, and giggled when Kingman held up his paw in greeting.

"See?" he said. "It just happened to me."

"What happened?" I asked, mystified.

"I just fell in love! With three girls in one go."

"You fell in love… with all of them?" I asked.

"Sure!"

I had a feeling that he'd fall out of love the moment the cats turned the corner. But then that's Kingman for you. In that sense he's not unlike his human, who also falls in and out of love like other people change their socks.

"So who do you think is the one for me, Kingman?" asked Dooley.

"I have no idea, Dooley. Isn't there someone special with whom you've felt the spark?"

"What spark?"

"The spark! You know—that tingly feeling? Butterflies in your tummy?"

But Dooley continued confused. "I like butterflies," he confessed. "They're pretty. But I'd never want to eat them."

"Of course not, Dooley," said Kingman, giving my friend a kindly pat on the back. "And a good thing, too. I bet butterflies don't like to be eaten, either."

"So what's eating Wilbur?" I asked, referring to the grumpy store owner.

"Oh, he's worried about the store again. Some rich guy has been making overtures to him about selling the place."

"What rich guy?"

"Joel Timperley? He owns the big mall over in Hampton Keys, and also a chain of supermarkets. And now he wants to lay his hands on the General Store and open a small version of his supermarket right here in this spot, which he reckons is prime real estate."

"I know Joel Timperley," I said. "We interviewed him earlier, about the murder of his bachelor friends."

"His family owns Timpermart, and they're rolling out a smaller version of their trademark giant supermarkets, designed to service the small-town shopper. The official line is that they want to revitalize Main Street, after they managed to destroy it by planting their Timpermarts and Timpermalls everywhere. The new project is called City Timpermart, and is like a miniature version of its big brother."

"And is Wilbur going to sell?"

"Of course not. He told Timperley over his dead body. But he's not the sole owner, is he? His brother Rudolph owns half, and since Rudolph's singing career isn't exactly taking off, he might be persuaded to sell his share."

"Is he still in LA?"

"No, he's touring. He joined a thrash metal band as their new lead singer. Last time we heard from him they were in Eastern Europe, and having a ball. Though they mainly play small venues, and not exactly making the big bucks."

"I doubt whether he'll ever break into the big time with thrash metal."

"No, thrash metal isn't exactly mainstream, is it?"

"Not unless Justin Bieber ventures into thrash metal."

"So maybe Wilbur is the one for you, Kingman," Dooley said, having giving the matter some thought. "He's a bachelor, and you're a bachelor, so you're perfect for each other."

"Oh, we are. We love living the bachelor life together, me and Wilbur," said Kingman with a grin. "In fact we love it so much, I hope we'll be together always."

"And Max and I love each other, too, so we're not bachelors, either."

"That's true," I admitted. "I do love you, buddy."

"And I love you, Max," said my friend fervently.

"In other words, a real lovefest," Kingman chuckled. He glanced around. "Where's Harriet and Brutus, by the way? Haven't seen those two lovebirds for a while."

"Max sent them on a mission," said Dooley. "They're spying on Omar Wissinski, along with Scarlett and Gran."

"Oh, you're sending them on missions now, are you?" said Kingman, arching an inquisitive whisker. "I never thought I'd see the day those two would do your bidding."

"They're not doing my bidding," I said. "We're a team, and

they're performing a vital task by keeping tabs on one of our main suspects in the case."

"Who are the other suspects?"

"A family named the Careens," I said, and proceeded to bring Kingman up to speed on our investigation.

"I know the Careens," he said. "Dominic Careen's got quite the temper on him."

"He does?" I asked.

"Absolutely. He was in here just last week, and when Wilbur informed him that he'd run out of Jonagolds, he kicked up a real fuss. Said it was a disgrace and even knocked over a couple of crates of oranges and then hit the wall so hard it left a big dent. I think Wilbur even decided to ban him from the shop for the time being—until he cools off."

"Why would he get so upset over Jonagolds?" I asked musingly.

"He said something about them being his wife's favorite apple."

"Interesting," I said. "If Dominic loses it over Jonagolds, I can't imagine what he'd do when he discovers the identity of the man who killed his daughter."

CHAPTER 20

That evening, Joel Timperley was working late as he often did, poring over projections for the coming fiscal quarter and going over some of the designs for the New Jersey mall, when he got a call on his mobile. He picked up with a casual, "Joel," and listened for a moment, then said, "Drop by the office, if you don't mind. I'll be here at least until ten."

After he hung up, he got up from behind his desk and wandered over to the model for the first mall the Timperleys ever built, and marveled at the progress they'd made over the years. That first mall was still the cornerstone of their retail empire, even though in comparison to the New Jersey mall, which would be the newest addition, it was small. Outdated, even. But he had grand plans for the Keystone Mall. He'd recently applied for an extension that would almost double its size, and add another few dozen stores. His granddad, if he were still alive today, would be proud, he was sure of it.

He glanced up when the elevator dinged, and his visitor joined him.

"Glad you could make it," he said. "I was just going over

some of the designs for the new—" But then he caught sight of the small shiny object in his visitor's hand.

There was a flash, and the shiny object suddenly lodged in his chest.

And as he gasped for air, he realized it was a knife, and he'd just been stabbed.

But then he toppled over, smashing the Keystone Mall model as he did.

CHAPTER 21

It rarely happens that the Keystone Mall closes, but today seemed to be one of those days. Of course there was a perfectly good reason: one of the cleaners who had arrived early that morning to start her working day had been happily scrubbing along, when all of a sudden she'd given the Zeus display a closer look and had discovered that a new figure had been added to the setup. Next to Zeus and his mortal enemy Dr. Ghoul a third figure had suddenly popped up, dressed in the kind of stretchy lycra outfit with added cape that seems to be all the rage with superheroes old and new, only this particular figure wasn't made of plastic, like the others, but was an actual living human being.

Though the living part was moot, since Joel Timperley was very obviously very dead.

The woman had screamed so loud her supervisor had come running, figuring there had been either a break-in or she'd seen a ghost. That or she'd used the wrong kind of detergent and had left spots on the marble floor.

Soon the police had arrived, along with an ambulance, but when the owner of the Keystone Mall had been declared dead, the mall had been closed down for the time being and all personnel had been gathered in the canteen to be interviewed one by one.

Not that they'd been able to provide a lot of useful information.

"So what have you got for us?" asked Chase as he stepped onto the scene.

"Single stab wound to the heart," said Abe Cornwall as he climbed down from the exhibit with some effort. "Very precise and very effective."

"Knife?"

"Looks like it. That or some other sharp instrument. I'll have to examine the wound more closely to be sure. Not a single drop of blood," the coroner continued, studying the body with a puzzled look on his round face, "so I doubt whether he was killed here."

"Killed elsewhere and dragged here, you think?"

"That would be my guess, yes. But as I said, I'll know more later."

"Time of death?"

"Sometime last night. I'd say between ten and midnight."

"That's the third bachelor in two days," said Odelia.

"Bad time for bachelors," said Abe, deadpan.

"Any CCTV?" Odelia asked.

"Somehow I have a feeling we won't get anything again," said Chase. "Let's talk to his parents first. They're waiting for us in the food court."

"The food court?"

"They both looked like they could use a cup of coffee."

So we walked over to the food court, the same spot where Gran had spent all day yesterday to receive Scarlett's reports. Today the court was completely empty, with the only two people occupying it a rather heavyset man and a rail-thin woman. Abraham and Miriam Timperley looked up hopefully when we arrived.

"Did you manage to save my boy?" asked Mr. Timperley.

"I'm afraid I have some bad news for you, sir," said Chase, not beating around the bush. "Joel didn't make it."

"My son… is dead?" asked the man, looking crestfallen all of a sudden.

"I'm afraid so. He died sometime last night."

"Oh, God," said Joel's mom as she clasped a desperate hand to her mouth.

Joel's dad, who'd half-risen, now dropped back into his chair like a bag of potatoes. "I don't believe this. Joel—dead. But… how?"

"He didn't die of natural causes."

"You mean he was… murdered?" Mr. Timperley almost whispered the words.

"Stabbed," said Chase. "And then placed in the Zeus display by the entrance."

"But who would do such a thing?"

"Oh, isn't it obvious?" asked Mrs. Timperley. "It's that family, of course. The Careens!" She spat out the word as if it was vile, which to her it probably was.

"Did the Careens formulate any threats to Joel?" asked Chase as he took a seat at the same table, followed by Odelia. Dooley and I, meanwhile, took up position one table over. With people in distress, you never know when they'll suddenly lash out or kick out, and it's always better to be safe than sorry.

"Not recently, but there was a time some years back when they used to come to the house, hurling all kinds of wild accusations at Joel."

"Who? Dominic? Or his son Rick?"

"Dominic Careen. Dreadful man. With a terrible temper.

He once threw a brick through a window. We had to get a restraining order against him. He stayed away after that."

"What did Joel have to say about it?" asked Odelia.

"Nothing much. Just that he had nothing to do with the death of the Careen girl," said Abraham. "And neither had any of his friends."

"Did you know that two of your son's friends have died?" asked Chase.

"Yes, Joel told us about it. Jona and Dunc. Horrible news. Joel was sick over it."

"Did he have any idea who might be behind their murders?"

"Dominic Careen, of course!" Abraham said. "Who else?"

"Apart from Dominic, did your son have any enemies that you know of?" asked Odelia. "Anyone who would wish him harm?"

"We have business competitors, but no one in their right mind would resort to violence to resolve a business conflict."

"Anyone in particular come to mind?" asked Chase, his pencil poised over his notebook.

Abraham thought for a moment, then slowly shook his head. "No one in particular, no," he said finally. "There were some issues with the New Jersey mall. Some of the neighbors lodged a complaint with the council against the plans, and one person refused to sell a piece of land. But we were going to build around it, no problem. Joel had the whole thing well in hand. In fact he was out there just last week, making some final arrangements, and the whole thing looks good to go."

"Did Joel ever mention a bachelor pact he made with Omar Wissinski, Sergio Sorbet, Dunc Hanover and Jona Morro?"

Miriam Timperley was pressing a piece of tissue to her nose, but shook her head. "That was all youthful nonsense as far as I'm concerned. Boy talk."

"Joel wasn't a teenager anymore, Mrs. Timperley," said Odelia softly.

"He was simply enjoying life as a single man," said Joel's dad.

"He was going to find the right girl soon enough," said his mom. "He was simply biding his time and taking advantage of his bachelor years."

"So you weren't worried that he'd never settle down and start a family?"

"Not in the least," said his father adamantly. "Joel was still young. He had plenty of time to settle down. He was sowing his wild oats."

"Did he have a girlfriend?"

"Nothing serious, no," his mom admitted.

"Joel was a handsome young man," said Abraham. "Successful and wealthy, too. He was very attractive to the ladies, and he took full advantage."

"But he didn't let it go to his head either," Miriam said, giving her husband a cautionary look. "He had a good head for business and his first focus were the Timpermart and Timpermall brands. He really wanted to expand the business and become the number one supermarket chain in the country."

"We're also making successful inroads into other markets," said Abraham. "Even overseas. As far as Joel was concerned, the sky was the limit." He heaved a deep sigh. "And now he's gone."

"Joel has a brother?"

"Yes, but he's not as interested in the business as Joel was. Johnny is a teacher, not a businessman."

"Though we've always been proud of both our boys," Miriam stressed.

"What's going to happen to the company now?" asked Chase.

Abraham shrugged. "Looks like I'll have to step in for now. And I guess we'll see how it goes. But I won't conceal the fact that Joel's death is a huge loss. A personal one but also for the company. He will be sorely missed." His face took on a note of hardness. "Please arrest Careen and that son of his, detective. Make sure they won't make any more victims."

"Sergio Sorbet?"

Abraham nodded. "I don't think it's a coincidence that our boy was left on that display. The killer was obviously trying to send a message. So at the very least you'll have to tell Sergio to get some security and make sure the Careens can't come anywhere near him."

CHAPTER 22

I'd told Odelia about what Kingman had said in regards to Wilbur Vickery, and she and Chase felt that it behooved them to pay a visit to the shop owner and find out about his whereabouts for the time of Joel Timperley's murder.

Wilbur seemed surprised that the police would think that he might have something to do with the death of the supermarket tycoon.

"Me!" he cried, tapping his puny chest with a bony fist. "A murderer! You must be out of your mind, Kingsley!"

"But it is true that Joel Timperley wanted to buy the store?"

"Yes, but that's no reason for me to kill him," said Wilbur.

We were in the store, which was temporarily closed while Kingman's human was being grilled by the police. Chase had first asked about the Jonagold incident, and had smoothly segued to the City Timpermart topic.

"Did the Timperleys also approach Rudolph?" asked Chase.

"I suppose they did."

"And isn't it true that Rudolph owns a fifty percent stake in both the store and the building?"

"Yes, but—"

"So if Rudolph decided to sell, that would put you in a difficult position?"

"Of course it would. Actually Rudolph doesn't own fifty percent but fifty-one percent. So if the Timperleys bought him out, they'd own the business outright. And it won't come as a surprise to you that they weren't going to keep the store running in its present form."

"What are their plans, did Joel say?"

"He made no secret of it. He wanted to turn the General Store into a so-called City Timpermart. It's a new concept they're launching, with smaller stores in city and town centers. The Hampton Cove City Timpermart would have been their pilot project, just like the Keystone Mall was the first mall the Timperleys built." He tapped his chest again, and raised his chin. "And I was going to have to sell to them cheap, because if I didn't, they'd buy up the property next door, and open a Timpermart right next to the General Store and drive me out of business with their cut-price tactics!"

"And what are the chances that Rudolph will sell?"

"I don't know," said Wilbur, dragging his fingers through his shaggy mane. "He's in Bulgaria right now, or Hungary, I'm not sure. Touring with his new band, you know."

"What's the name of the band?" asked Odelia, amused.

"Um, Satan's Brood, I think. They're pretty awful, I can tell you. And not very successful. So there's every chance that Rudolph will want to sell out. Provided the Timperleys have managed to reach him. When he's touring, Rudolph isn't always available for business conferences." He grinned, his crooked yellow teeth bare. "He lives in a bottle, most of the time, though he likes to refer to it as living with his muse."

"Where were you last night between ten and midnight, Wilbur?" asked Chase.

"I was here. Well, upstairs. Watching television."

"Can anyone confirm that?"

"Kingman can."

Both Dooley and I glanced over to Kingman, who'd sat listening to the conversation intently. He now gave us a nod of confirmation. "Yep, he was right here with me, all right."

"Are you sure, Kingman?" I asked. "You don't have to cover for him if you don't want to."

"No, but he was here. I'm not going to lie to you about something like that, am I?"

I studied our friend closely, and when I saw no signs of deception, I gave Odelia the nod. She transferred that nod to Chase, and the cop seemed satisfied.

It was probably the first time in the history of law enforcement that a cat had been able to provide his human with a solid alibi, and that the alibi had been accepted. Though if questioned in court, I very much doubt whether Kingman's testimony would have stood up to cross-examination.

"What do you think will happen now?" asked Wilbur. "With the plans, I mean?"

"I don't know, Wilbur," said Chase honestly. "Looks like Abraham Timperley will come out of retirement now that his son is dead. Though from what he told us he seems more preoccupied with a new mall they're building in New Jersey than your store."

"I'd still try to get in touch with your brother," said Odelia, "and convince him not to sell to the Timperleys."

"Fat lot of good that'll do me. Rudolph has never been one to listen to me."

"So maybe you could make him a business proposition? Buy him out?"

"With what? I don't have that kind of money."

Chase clapped the small business owner on the back. "I'm sure you'll figure it out."

"Not unless I win the lottery," Wilbur grumbled.

"Or you could reach some kind of arrangement with the Timperleys," said Odelia. "Go into business with them. In exchange you'll stay on here at the General Store."

"And become some local stooge for corporate greed? No, thank you very much. I've always been my own boss, and I'm not about to change that."

Kingman gave us a grin. "That's my human for you. Stubborn to the last."

"I hope he'll be able to save his store," I said. "Otherwise you'll have to go."

Kingman's face sagged. "Yeah, I know. So you see? Wilbur would never kill Joel Timperley. He's not stupid. He knows that chopping off one head of the Hydra doesn't change a thing. It just grows a new head and becomes even more vicious!"

I'd never heard anyone refer to the Timperleys as a multi-headed monster, but maybe Kingman was right. Wilbur was no fool, and murdering one scion of that powerful family wouldn't make one ounce of difference to their long-term plans. All it might accomplish was to slow down their expansion, buying Wilbur time to think up a solution.

In spite of Kingman's wholehearted endorsement of his human, somehow I wasn't a hundred percent convinced he wouldn't lie for Wilbur. He was that fond of him.

On the other hand, it now looked as if the murder of Joel Timperley was connected to the murders of his two bachelor friends, and even though Wilbur might have had a motive to kill Joel, I couldn't see anything that connected him to Jona Morro or Dunc Hanover.

So Wilbur was off the hook.

At least for now.

But Wilbur wouldn't be a small business owner if he didn't have one parting shot to impart. He leaned in and fixed Chase with beady little eyes. "If you really want to find out who killed Joel Timperley I suggest you go and talk to Jeannie Beaton."

"The mayor of Hampton Keys?"

Wilbur nodded ominously. "The Timperleys are in the middle of a rebranding operation. Joel told me they're going to rename the Keystone Mall and call it Timpermall from now on, dropping the 'Keys' from the name. And I have it on good authority that that didn't sit well with the Hampton Keys council. Not well at all."

CHAPTER 23

Jeannie Beaton was a short woman of stocky build, with a rugged and ruddy face. She didn't look like a mayor to me, but then there probably aren't any requirements for a mayor's outward appearance as far as I know. She certainly didn't look as refined and pretty as Charlene Butterwick, our own mayor.

Mayor Beaton was seated behind a large desk that dwarfed her, and I had the impression she'd had to get an extra-high chair so she wouldn't disappear from view.

"Poppycock," she now said with an indulgent smile. "We're still in negotiations with the Timperleys about the new name for the mall."

"So there will be a new name?" asked Chase.

"Well, obviously, since they own the mall, they can name it whatever they want. But we as the town council also have a say in this. This is our town, after all, and we do have some leverage we can bring to bear on the business owners who want to operate a store on our territory."

"In other words: if the Timperleys don't want to play ball, you can cause trouble for them."

"Not trouble, per se," said the Mayor, weighing her words carefully. "But we do have some instruments in our arsenal that might convince them not to be rash when taking such a drastic decision."

"So what was your suggestion?" asked Odelia. "That they keep the same name?"

"I actually talked to Joel last week, and I suggested that they name the mall Timpermall Hampton Keys. Or even Hampton Keys Timpermall. With or without a hyphen."

"And was he amenable to your suggestion?" asked Odelia with a smile.

The Mayor returned the smile and added some wattage of her own. "I think he was starting to come round to our way of thinking. After all, the Keystone Mall has been an integral part of this town for the past fifty years, and I conveyed the message to Joel that we were hoping to keep hosting the mall on our territory for many years to come."

"And what did he say?"

Her smile faltered a little. "That Hampton Cove was also interested in operating a mall on their territory, and so was Happy Bays. Then again," she added, the smile fully in evidence again, "you don't simply relocate an entire mall. It would have cost them a small fortune. So chances are that we're going to win this battle, and soon we'll be able to host the Timpermall Hampton Keys—the most likely compromise and one we can fully endorse." She shrugged. "Between you and me, I never liked the name Keystone Mall. We aren't the Keystone Cops, after all, and Keystone sounds so... Stone Age, don't you think?"

Chase didn't let on what he thought of the name, if he had an opinion about it at all. "I have to ask you this, Madam Mayor, but where were you last night between ten and midnight?"

111

"Goodness me," said Mayor Beaton, bringing a hand to her chest. "Am I a suspect now?"

"Just routine," Chase clarified. "This way we can eliminate you from our inquiries."

"Eliminate me! I don't know if I like that term," the Mayor quipped, then turned serious. "Actually I was dining with a friend last night."

"Do you have a name and phone number for me?" asked Chase, taking out his notebook.

"Of course. Charlene Butterwick," she said, and gave a surprised-looking Chase a look of triumph. "Us small-town mayors like to stay in touch. United we stand and all that."

"Were you by any chance discussing the rebranding?" asked Chase dryly.

"The topic might have come up," said the Mayor. "And for your information, Charlene isn't interested in a new mall on her territory any more than I am of losing one. So there goes your motive flying right out of the window!" And she laughed a hearty laugh.

Once outside, Chase placed a call to his boss, who placed a call to his girlfriend, and moments later we were in a conference call with Charlene Butterwick.

"Yes, I had Jeannie over for dinner last night," Charlene confirmed. "And also Ted MacDonald, the mayor of Happy Bays. We thought it would be a good idea to join forces now that the Timperleys are trying to drive a wedge between us and use brute force to push through their ideas."

"I see," said Chase. "What ideas?"

"They want to expand the mall. Double its size, actually. But they're having some trouble convincing people this is a good idea. And so they've been trying to bully council members and some of the farmers who own the land they want to buy into submission."

"So not just a rebranding but also an expansion?"

"The rebranding would go hand in hand with the expansion."

"And what are the chances that their plans will see the light of day?"

"I'd say their chances are pretty good, but they're not going to get everything they want. There will have to be some modifications, and Joel was negotiating with Jeannie and the Hampton Keys council and frankly driving a hard bargain, which is why Jeannie thought it a good idea for the three mayors to get together and decide on a joint strategy."

"Do you think Joel's death is beneficial to the council's position?" asked Chase.

"I don't think it's going to make a lot of difference either way. No, I'm afraid you're barking up the wrong tree here, Chase. We didn't kill Joel Timperley. Though I have to admit we were all tempted, Jeannie most of all."

"Got any more questions for my future wife, Chase?" asked Uncle Alec.

There was silence on the line, then suddenly Odelia cried, "Oh, my God!"

Charlene laughed. "Alec! I thought we said we'd wait until this weekend!"

"Oops," Uncle Alec said, suddenly subdued. "Looks like the cat's out of the bag now."

Dooley gave me a curious look. "What cat are they talking about, Max? And why a bag?"

"It's just an expression, Dooley," I said. "There's no cat and no bag."

"Strange expression," said my friend. "A little cruel, if you ask me."

"Well, I guess congratulations are in order," said Odelia.

"Thanks, hon," said Charlene. "We'll celebrate later, all right?"

"Of course."

"Yeah, first catch this killer," said Uncle Alec sternly. "Have you talked to Sergio Sorbet yet?"

"We're going over there now," said Chase.

"Better get a move on. Before he ends up dead, too!"

"Ooh, can you get me an autograph?" asked Charlene. "Tell him to make it 'With love to Charlene!'"

Even mayors aren't immune to the charms of Hollywood leading men, apparently, even small-town mayors that are about to get married to small-town chiefs of police!

CHAPTER 24

The house that Sergio Sorbet had built—or rather bought—was a grand mansion in true Hollywood style. I imagined that Steven Spielberg was a regular guest, and so was Tom Hanks and Harrison Ford. They probably landed their helicopter on the private helipad Sergio had installed between the house and his private beach. Or maybe they flew in their private plane and landed it at the private airstrip nearby. All in all, it all sounded very… private. Then again, when you're as rich and famous as Mr. Sorbet, you don't like mere mortals sticking their noses into your private affairs.

The movies that had made Sorbet famous were very much in evidence wherever we looked: a large Zeus statue dominated the courtyard, and a ginormous painting of Zeus covered the two floors of the atrium when we entered. There was even a mosaic floor depicting a scene from one of the Zeus movies—at least I thought it did. I've never personally been a big fan of the Zeus franchise. It all seems a little samey, to me, in the sense that when you've seen one, you've seen them all. But I guess that's the whole point.

"Come in, come in," said Sergio Sorbet once we'd made it

past two security guards, one butler and one helpful personal assistant or PA, who appeared to have a tablet glued to his hand and an earpiece to his ear.

Sergio himself was a large man, and seemed to have been constructed entirely of muscle. He had a thick neck, brawny arms that stretched a Zeus T-shirt and bulging pectoral muscles that reminded me of that old *Incredible Hulk* TV series from the eighties, where Bill Bixby was always in danger of suddenly ripping his shirt to shreds and turning into Lou Ferrigno. They must have gone through an awful lot of shirts to film that particular series.

Sergio looked a little sweaty, but immediately explained this by stating that he'd been engaged in his second workout of the day, and a particularly grueling one at that.

"I shift tractor tires," he said, as if it was the most obvious thing in the world.

"Tractor tires?" asked Odelia.

"Yeah. Best workout possible. Exercises chest, back, arm, leg muscles. Whole-body workout. But you're not here to talk about my exercise regimen, are you?" He gave us the good-natured smile he was famous for, oozing charm from every sweaty pore.

"Have you heard about what happened to Joel Timperley, sir?" asked Chase.

The man's face fell. "Yeah, Luke told me. My PA," he clarified. "Terrible business. Simply terrible. Have you arrested the man yet?"

"What man?" asked Chase.

"Why, Dominic Careen, of course. He must be the one behind all this, right?"

"What makes you say that?"

"Isn't it obvious? That entire family has been pestering us for years. And now three of my friends are dead and you're

116

telling me you haven't picked him up yet? What are you waiting for, man?"

"We're waiting until we have solid evidence of Dominic Careen's involvement," said Chase. "And until we do, I'm afraid our hands are tied."

"Well, I'm not taking any chances. I've doubled my guard detail, and if Careen wants to kill me next, he's got another thing coming. In fact I've handed out the man's picture to all of my security people, and told them to shoot first and ask questions later."

"I strongly advise against that, sir," said Chase decidedly.

"I'm not asking for your advice, detective. I have to think about my safety now. There's a madman out there who's already killed three times, and it's pretty obvious I'm next."

"What if I told you that we have solid evidence that suggests that your friend Dunc Hanover was the person driving the car that killed Mr. Careen's daughter?"

The action hero frowned, a thing he did so well in his movies. In fact he was almost always frowning, as his main enemy Dr. Ghoul was always trying to kill him. Not unlike Dominic Careen, apparently—or at least according to the superhero actor. "I don't understand. We were nowhere near the street where that little girl was killed. We've told the police time and time again. What is this evidence?"

"A detailed account the garage owner who fixed Mr. Hanover's car the morning after the accident kept. It clearly states the work he carried out to hide all evidence of the accident."

"I'm sure there must be some mistake," said the beefy actor, flexing his muscles, out of sheer habit, I assumed.

"He's very big, isn't he, Max?" said Dooley. "He probably eats a lot of potatoes."

"I don't think it's potatoes that made him this big, Dooley. He exercises a lot."

"Chase also exercises a lot, but compared to Sergio, Chase is tiny."

"I wouldn't exactly call Chase tiny." But it was true that next to Sergio, Chase did indeed look small. And judging from the cop's testy questions, he didn't like it.

"No mistake," said Chase. "It's clearly Dunc Hanover's car."

"Then there must have been some other collision he was involved in that night. We were always hitting stuff. If you're going to engage in street races some minor damage is to be expected. And we weren't very precious about our cars, detective—not in the least."

"What did surprise me is that Dunc owned a Mustang. That's a pretty expensive car for a man with modest means."

Sergio smiled. "I remember that Mustang. A great machine. Dunc was really proud of that car. He got it secondhand, actually, with a little help from his friends, of course."

"You bought him that car?"

"We all chipped in. You see, Dunc's folks didn't have the kind of funds at their disposal that the rest of us had, but we still considered him one of us. So when we got into cars, we felt he had to have a car of his own, just like the rest of us. And since it was obvious he couldn't afford it, we created a pool and got him that Mustang."

"So you claim that his Mustang was in an accident that night but not involving Poppy Careen."

Sergio sighed as he impatiently tapped the back of the couch. "How many times do I have to say this. We had nothing to do with what happened to the girl. And now if you'll excuse me, I have a hot date with a protein shake." And abruptly he got up and disappeared.

"He has a hot date with a protein shake?" asked Dooley. "I thought he was a bachelor?"

"I think bachelors are allowed to cheat on the bachelor code with protein, Dooley."

"So what do you think?" asked Chase, leaning forward.

"I think we're not going to get Scarlett and Charlene and Mom their autographs."

Chase shook his head. "Not Marge, too!"

"I'm afraid so," said Odelia with a grin.

"I don't believe this. He's just some actor!"

"Yeah, but what an actor."

"Oh, God. Not you, too, babe."

Odelia shrugged. "I happen to like the Zeus movies. They're very… entertaining."

Sergio had returned, and I could see traces of a pink substance on his lips. Presumably his protein shake was of the strawberry variety. "Are we done here?" he asked. "I have to rest now. In one hour I have another workout to put in. Ropes, this time."

"Ropes?" asked Odelia, her eyes caressing the man's impressive torso.

"Yeah, you know." He made a yanking motion with both hands, bending at the knees as he did. "Battle ropes. Great workout. You must have done some rope work, detective. You look like a man who knows his way around a gym."

"I work out," Chase confirmed. "Though not as much as you, obviously."

"This is what I do," said Sergio. "In fact it's all I do. All day, every day."

"Must be tough," said Chase, and he seemed to mean it.

"Yeah, well. It pays good money, so…"

"Will you be in town long?" asked Chase, changing the subject.

"It was supposed to be just this week. Premiere of the new movie. But now it looks like I'll stick around for the funerals." He fixed Chase with a manly frown. "My three best friends. All dead. And you're sitting there grilling me about some old Mustang Dunc used to drive. Get out there, man, and catch that killer." He was pointing to the door, and the message was clear. "And stop wasting time!" he suddenly thundered—in true Zeus style.

So we got up and made to leave. Odelia opened her lips to ask about those autographs, but Sergio Sorbet had sunk down on the couch again, and had assumed the position of Rodin's The Thinker, complete with bulging bicep. He was glowering, and for all intents and purposes looked like a man who was about to launch a bolt of lightning at us.

So Odelia closed her mouth again. Looked like Scarlett, Charlene and Marge would have to do without any love from their favorite action hero for now.

We walked out of the house and looked up at the sky. Clouds were gathering overhead, and it looked as if a storm was brewing. The wind had picked up, and was making some stray leaves spin around on the courtyard where our car was parked. In the distance thunder rumbled, and I thought I could see a flash of lightning slice the sky.

Clearly the god of thunder and lightning was not a happy camper.

CHAPTER 25

In spite of the impending storm, we decided to head out that night. Cat choir is not for the faint of heart, after all, and not even a storm can stop us from gathering at the park to get together and sing our hearts out.

Also, I was hoping to get Shanille's point of view on this recent spate of murders. She is, after all, a very spiritual being, being Father Reilly's cat and all, and might have an original viewpoint on the whole sordid affair.

On the walk over to the park, Harriet told us some more about what had happened at the mall that day. After the police had released the crime scene, the mall had quickly reopened for business, and even Omar Wissinski had reopened his shop.

"He was very sad, though," said Harriet.

"Yeah, he looked white as a sheet," said Brutus.

"I don't think he's fully recovered from that knock on the head. In fact he probably should have stayed home in bed— or the hospital to have his head looked at."

"Scarlett thinks he has a concussion, which is why he's been acting so strange."

"Strange, how?" I asked.

"Well, today his mother came in again, and they argued about Argyle."

"His brother?"

Brutus nodded. "His younger brother. Looks like he and Omar don't get along."

"Omar has a really hard time," said Harriet. "Three of his best friends are dead now, and he almost died, too."

"He's scared they'll come back to finish the job," Brutus clarified. "So he's hired a security guard."

"A security guard?" I asked.

"Yeah. He arrived this morning, and stayed posted at the door all day. Just like you see in jewelry stores."

"But Omar is afraid he'll scare away the customers, so he hopes Chase will arrest Dominic Careen soon."

"So he thinks Dominic is behind these murders, too, does he?"

"Yeah, either Dominic or the gambling mafia. Though what are the odds that three of Omar's friends had gambling debts?"

"It's possible, of course," I said. "It's not because they're rich that they're not also gamblers. A lot of people these days gamble online, which has lowered the threshold and has removed the social stigma associated with gambling. If you visit a casino, someone might see you, or snap your picture. But if you gamble online, from the safety of your own home, there's nobody to name and shame you, and it has made the gambling industry go through a real boom."

"I don't know," said Harriet. "I still think it's Dominic Careen and his son who are behind all of this. It takes a lot of strength to make a car crash down on a person, or to turn a person into a papier-mâché statue, or even to turn him into a display figure, like in Joel Timperley's case. Has Chase figured out how they killed Mr. Timperley yet?"

"Yeah, they found blood in his office and in the elevator. And the big model of the Keystone Mall was crushed and also had blood on it. So it looks like Joel was killed there, and then taken down to the atrium to be strung up as part of the new Zeus movie display."

"It's all so, so terrible," said Harriet. "And I, for one, hope they'll catch the killer before he kills Sergio Sorbet. That man is so..." She was going to say more, but caught Brutus's eye and wisely swallowed her next words.

We'd arrived at the park, and made our way to the playground, which is our domain by night. Most cats had decided to show up, with only a few scared off by the impending storm. I made a beeline for Shanille, eager to consult with her.

"Hey, Max," she said, looking busy. She probably had been thinking up new songs for her choir to interpret. "How is the investigative business going? Catch any killers lately?"

"Not really," I said. "We're three murders in, and not a clue as to the killer or killers."

"Oh?" she said, a little distracted as she surveyed her troops. "Looks like some of our members have decided to skip tonight's rehearsal," she said censoriously.

"Yeah, I guess they don't want to get caught in the storm."

"What storm?"

I pointed up, where the tree branches were swaying in a powerful wind and the night had turned fully pitch black by now. "That storm."

"Oh, that. Just a little wind, that's all. Your true cat choir enthusiast doesn't let that deter him from his true passion. Now you were saying something about your case?"

"Yeah, three people have been killed so far, but the evidence is pointing in different directions." And so I explained to her about the difficult case we were dealing with.

"Well, it's obvious who's behind this, isn't it?" she said finally, after hearing me out.

"It is?" I said, much surprised. Was it possible I'd over-looked the obvious?

"God is striking down these men," said Shanille, as if it was the most logical thing.

"God?" I asked, and inadvertently my eyes slid upward to the sky above, where presumably the Big Man was looking down on us mere felines.

"Of course! They're all confirmed bachelors, you say? Refusing to get married?"

"Yes, all except—"

"So of course the good Lord would strike them down, setting an example." She eyed me with a look of amusement. "You can't expect to go against God's will and not suffer the consequences, Max. It simply doesn't work like that."

"But one of them—"

"Of course God didn't *personally* set out to kill them. But one of his servants did. So you have to look for a person or persons who firmly believes that every man and woman should be joined in holy matrimony, and if they don't? Well, they brought it on themselves, didn't they?"

"That's a pretty harsh view," I said, after giving this novel theory some thought.

"It's the only possible explanation. And now you'll have to excuse me, Max. I have to get this unruly bunch in line for tonight's rehearsal!"

As she did just that, I wondered about her words. There was of course one fatal flaw in her reasoning: one man had indeed decided to engage in holy matrimony. Dunc Hanover had been on the verge of the married state, and he, too, had been struck down.

So not the wrath of God after all?

Dooley had joined me. "Looks like it's going to rain, Max,"

he said nervously. "Maybe we should go. I hate to get wet. I really do."

"All cats hate to get wet, Dooley," I said. Just then, the first big drop of rain fell down, right on top of my nose. Yikes!

"It's raining, Max!" my friend cried.

"Yeah, I can see that," I grunted, and then we made a straight line for the nearest tree, which would give us some protection at least. And as we sheltered there, soon more cats joined us, and also under the other trees surrounding the playground.

Shanille wasn't deterred, though. Shouting to make herself heard over the sound of the pounding rain and the wind that had picked up, she screamed, "Let's not let a little bit of rain stop us from doing what is in fact our holy mission, people! Let's sing our hearts out, my fellow friends! And take it from the top!"

So she held up her arms just so, and then we all launched into a rather unenthusiastic rendition of 'Raindrops keep falling on my head.' It seemed particularly appropriate.

CHAPTER 26

Odelia had been sleeping more or less peacefully, when a deep voice raised her from her slumber. It was Chase, and he accompanied his words with a gentle shake.

"What is it?" she muttered sleepily.

"Just got a call," said her husband, looking just as sleepy as she did.

"God, not another murder!" she said, instantly wide awake.

"The fire department, actually," said Chase. "Something about cats in a tree."

Her eyes flashed to the foot of the bed, and when she saw that Max and Dooley weren't there, her heart skipped a beat. "Let's go," she said, and immediately swung her feet from under the duvet.

It was chilly out, and as they drove over to the park, where the person who'd called Chase had directed them, she wrapped her jacket more closely around herself.

"I hope they're all right," she said.

"I'm sure they are fine," Chase reassured her. "They're cats. They always land on their feet."

"Hm," she said quietly, sinking a little deeper in her seat. This whole murder business was starting to take its toll on her. Especially the fact that they didn't seem to be getting any closer to identifying the killer. Pressure was mounting, but there were only so many hours in the day, and already they were using all of them to trace this elusive killer.

"We need to talk to the garage owner," she reminded Chase. "Jefferson Gusta."

"Way ahead of you, babe," Chase grunted. "Jefferson Gusta died last month, but his son Vince took over the business. I've arranged to meet him first thing."

"And we have to talk to the Careens again."

"And we will. First let's get your cats out of that tree."

"I wonder what made them get up that tree in the first place."

"Have you seen the weather?" asked Chase.

She had. In fact rain was lashing the windscreen now, the wipers working at full speed and still not able to remove the water fast enough to provide a clear view of the road. Suddenly lightning slashed the night sky, and lit up the road in eerie clarity, immediately followed by a crashing thunder that seemed to shake the earth and rattle the car.

"It's right over Hampton Cove," she said. "My cats will be so scared. They hate storms."

"We're almost there," he assured her. "Did you bring the umbrella?"

She nodded, though a measly umbrella wouldn't do much good against the elements this storm had unleashed. The rain was hitting them from every direction, not simply falling down in a straight vertical line as it should.

The lights of several fire trucks guided them to the place where the trouble centered, and Chase parked his pickup right behind the nearest one. They got out, and immediately were pummeled by a gale-force wind. A branch had snapped off a tree and was lying across the road.

"This is getting pretty dangerous!" Chase cried over the otherworldly roar from the storm. He was holding up the umbrella, until suddenly it simply snapped up and flew off!

They trudged on, hair whipped by the storm, and faces pummeled by sluicing rain.

Finally they arrived at the playground, which was where the cats liked to gather at night, to gab and sing their hearts out, much to the annoyance of the park's neighbors.

"I don't see them!" she cried, as she looked around. But then Chase pointed up, and as she glanced in the direction he was pointing, suddenly she saw it: dozens and dozens of cats, all up in the trees that lined the playground, and all looking absolutely terrified!

The fire department had set up powerful halogen lights, and pointed them at those trees, and caught in the glare of those lights, dozens of cat eyes reflected back, wide and black and fearful!

She searched for her own cats, and suddenly a familiar pitiful mewling reached her ears. It was Max, and he looked fully soaked to the skin, as did Dooley, clutching to the same tree branch. Next to them, Harriet and Brutus were also holding on for dear life!

"Oh, my treasures!" she cried, and reached up to them. But of course they were too far up. "They'll never be able to get down from there!" she yelled to Chase.

"We'll have to go and get them," he said, and hurried over to a nearby fireman.

And as she watched, she saw that the fire department was getting ready to mount an operation to get those cats out of those trees pronto, with several ladder trucks being positioned to accomplish that complicated task.

"I never thought I'd say this," a fireman yelled as he joined her, "but I'm actually more nervous to go up there than to head into a burning building!"

"And why is that!" she asked.

"Because it's cats! And no matter what you do, they will fight you every step of the way, even if all you're doing is trying to save them! And of course there's that!" He was pointing to a nearby tree, which saw a branch dangerously sweeping in the wind. "That's gonna go down any minute!"

On the branch, several cats were hanging on and looking terrified.

"Just do your best," she said. "I'll try to calm them down."

He grinned at her. "I know you will, Mrs. Kingsley. That's why we called you in!"

Oh, dear. She really was the town's cat lady, wasn't she?

And while the ladders were being slowly extended, and the fire personnel got ready to mount them, she yelled, "These brave people are going to come and save you! So please cooperate as best you can. And that means no scratching, no clawing, and whatever you do, don't try to be cute and climb even higher into those trees! That goes for you, too, Buster!"

The cats all seemed to pay attention, and when Max repeated her message, she was starting to believe this rescue operation might just be pulled off without any casualties. But when the first fireman had reached the first cat, the feline suddenly hauled off and smacked him right on the helmet!

"Tigger, no!" suddenly an authoritative voice bellowed. "You will cooperate! Now!"

"Yes, Harriet," the cat named Tigger said meekly, and allowed the fireman to grab him and one of his fellow cats, and take him down.

"All of you!" Harriet boomed in a surprisingly powerful voice. "If you don't behave, you'll have me to deal with! And if you think this storm is bad, wait until I come for you!"

"Yes, Harriet," several more voices called out. "We'll be good, Harriet!"

And so it happened. The firefighters fought the storm, and their own fear of being clawed or bitten or scratched, and one by one all the cats of Hampton Cove were brought down from those trees. It was a rescue operation worthy of a disaster movie starring Chris Pratt or Dwayne Johnson, and when the last cat had been safely returned to earth, a loud cheer rose up. It was the cats' way of paying tribute to their heroic saviors.

And it didn't even sound out of tune.

Odelia was soon reunited with Max and Dooley and Harriet and Brutus, and she hugged them all as they clung to her fiercely.

"You did well, you guys," she said, a little thickly. "Especially you, Harriet."

"Just doing my bit," Harriet said modestly. Then she added, a little less modestly, "A queen has to rule, so that's what I did."

"I was really scared, Odelia," said Dooley.

Just then, a loud creaking sound had them all look up, and before their very eyes, the branch that had been precariously swaying in the wind, now tore off that tree and crashed down on top of the jungle gym, flattening it as it did.

The four cats looked on with fear written all over their features.

"And to think we were sitting on that thing only an hour ago," said Max softly.

"Is this the end of cat choir, Max?" asked Dooley.

"I don't know, Dooley, but it's certainly the end of that jungle gym."

In fact the whole playground infrastructure seemed badly damaged. The swing was down, as were the slide, the merry-go-round and the seesaw.

"Let's go home," she said. "There's nothing we can do here."

They'd have to return in the morning, to assess the damage.

The cats didn't have to be told twice, and so they all hurried to the car, to be out of the rain, which was still lashing their faces, and the wind, whipping the trees above. Most of all she was afraid another branch would be torn loose, and flatten either them or the car.

The fire department, too, was urging everyone to leave the area.

Chase wiped the rain from his eyes and stuck his key into the ignition. "The fire chief told me the park had been closed off, but a couple of the neighbors heard the cats cry out, and called it in. They said they made a sound like they never heard before."

"Scared to death, the poor darlings," said Odelia as she hugged her cats close.

"We should have kept them at home," said Chase as he crunched the car in gear.

"I know—but I had no idea it would get this bad." Also, it's very hard to tell cats what to do. And apart from locking the cat flap, it wasn't easy to make them stay home.

At least they'd learned their lesson: don't venture out in a raging storm.

"I'm so happy we're still alive," said Dooley. "I was so scared."

"Brutus was singing for us," said Max. "It was very nice."

"I always sing when I'm scared," said Brutus. "It helps."

"You were scared, too?" asked Dooley, much surprised.

"Of course."

"I didn't think you ever got scared," said Dooley.

"Every cat gets scared sometimes, Dooley. No matter what they tell you."

"You have a nice singing voice, Brutus," said Max. "Very soothing."

"Thanks, buddy," said Brutus.

Arriving home, they ushered the cats inside, and she rubbed them dry with big, coarse towels until they practically glowed, then she planted them in front of an electric heater, and she and Chase went upstairs to take a hot shower.

By the time the whole family was back in bed, it was two o'clock.

And while the storm raged outside, soon they were all out like a light.

CHAPTER 27

Sergio Sorbet didn't mind the rain, or the wind or even the thunder and lightning. In fact he reveled in it! He was, after all, used to playing Zeus, and after seven years and four movies, he'd almost started believing that he was, in fact, the famous Greek god.

So he stood in the rain on top of the flat roof of the house, and screamed into the wind, holding his powerful arms aloft and defying the elements.

It invigorated him. He drew strength from it—he loved it!

He roared again, raising his face to the sky. Above him, the weather gods raged and rampaged but the more they castigated the earth, the louder he screamed back.

"I am Zeus!" he boomed, his voice drowned out by the wind.

From somewhere up there, he thought he heard the sound of laughter.

So he let out a loud roar and pummeled his chest.

"I AM ZEUS!"

Suddenly, he felt a stinging pain against his left temple, and briefly wondered if he'd been hit by a pellet of hail. He shook his head like a dog, then experienced another hit, harder this time, and momentarily lost his balance and sank down to his knees, his hands hitting the water that stood, ankle deep, all across the roof, the gutters and drainpipes unable to handle the sheer volume.

When the third hit came, this time to the back of his head, he went down hard.

And didn't come up again.

Jasmine Muchari had been in the Sorbet family's employ as a housekeeper for going on thirty years now. She'd been there in the good days, the bad days, and everything in between. Lately the Sorbets had only experienced good days, though, especially since their son had become a global superstar, his movies grossing billions. In fact ever since he'd been cast as Zeus, Sergio had gone through an impressive transformation. Gone were the boozy weekends with his dubious friends, or the late-night dates with questionable women. These days all he did was spend hours in the gym, sculpting a physique that could only be called godly.

So when she entered the man's bedroom, she fully expected him to be up already, and slaving away in the home gym he'd built. It wasn't unusual for Sergio to get up at five o'clock or even four, to start on the first of several workouts spread throughout the day.

Jasmine had always thought that the life of an actor consisted of studying their lines and declamating them in front of a mirror. But apparently the life of the modern actor was dominated by protein drinks and energy drinks and grueling workouts and lots and lots of selfies taken of bulging muscles and sweaty brows and shared with millions of fans.

When she didn't see a sign of Sergio in the bedroom, she smiled with satisfaction. But when she saw that his bed hadn't been slept in, that smile disappeared. Her employer needed his sleep. Many was the time he'd demanded no one disturb him so he could get his eight hours in. Those huge muscles only bulked up when granted sufficient rest.

She walked out of the bedroom and almost bumped into that horrible little man who called himself a PA. Luke Grimsby was wearing those red-framed glasses again, which gave him the look of a pompous art gallery owner. He had his nose glued to his tablet, as usual. It was where he kept track of Sergio's training schedule, and also his nutrition schedule, both equally important, apparently.

"Where's Sergio?" she asked.

"No idea," Luke muttered as he adjusted his glasses and peered at her as if seeing her for the first time. He did this every time, the supercilious fool. "In the gym, probably."

"He didn't go to bed last night."

The PA wrinkled his nose, causing his glasses to shift up. "What do you mean?"

"I mean he didn't go to bed."

"Impossible. Sergio knows how important it is to—"

"Look for yourself, Luke. His bed hasn't been slept in."

Luke hurried into the room. "But… I saw him go up last night."

"Up where?"

"The roof. He wanted to experience the storm firsthand. Said it inspired him. And also, he wanted to take a selfie for his Insta." He locked eyes with Jasmine. "You don't think…"

The words hung between them. Then, as one person, they both turned on their heel and quickly made their way to the staircase that ran to the roof.

"How could you let him go out there!" Jasmine cried.

"You know Sergio. The man loves a good storm!"

135

They arrived on the roof, and Jasmine glanced around. The chimney stack was there, the parapet lining the roof, the antenna as it pointed straight up into the sky, and as her eyes drifted past the antenna and back to the chimney stack, scanning the tar roof floor, suddenly something clicked in her brain. She'd registered some anomaly. Something that wasn't as it should be.

Slowly her eyes swiveled back to the antenna.

And that's when she saw it: strapped to the antenna was a large object. Dark and bulky, with strips of material flapping in the light breeze that had followed last night's fierce storm. And as she took in more details, suddenly she heard a cry. She didn't realize at first that it was she who'd uttered it, just as it took her mind a few seconds to come to terms with the information her eyes were sending it.

It was Sergio Sorbet.

Strapped to the antenna.

And fully burned to a crisp.

CHAPTER 28

It seemed like it was only yesterday that we were out at Sergio Sorbet's house, talking to the man, and that's because it was indeed only yesterday that we were out there.

Now we were back, and this time we were on the roof of Sergio's property, staring at the actor, who looked a little bit less like a superhero today than he had yesterday.

"What happened to him?" asked Dooley.

"Looks like he was hit by lightning," I said. "More than once."

"Why would he do a thing like that?" asked my friend.

"I don't think he did it on purpose, Dooley. I think he was strapped to that antenna and left there to die."

"But didn't he know it's very dangerous to be struck by lightning? Not to mention unhealthy?"

"I think he was murdered."

"Murdered!"

"Yep. Murdered by lightning." I had to think back to Shanille's words last night: how God was punishing all those bachelors for their sin of refusing to get married. But this was taking that punishment up to a whole new level.

"So what do you think, Abe?" asked Chase.

The paunchy coroner looked down from his lofty position next to the fallen action star. "I'm thinking this has got to stop, Kingsley. This is, what, the fourth murder in four days?"

"Tell that to the killer. He was killed, right?"

"Oh, absolutely. Received a series of nasty blows to the head which would almost certainly have rendered him unconscious, then tied to the antenna in the hope he'd be struck by lightning. And since we experienced one of the worst storms in a decade last night, I think the murderer would have been pleased. Poor guy was hit repeatedly, I'd say."

"So he was killed by lightning."

"Yeah, pretty much killed him immediately, I reckon. And then was struck a number of times more after that." He gestured for his people to take the body of the unfortunate actor down, as he clambered down with some difficulty himself.

"Ironic," said Odelia. "The god of lightning killed by lightning."

"All of these deaths have been ironic," said Chase. "The joyrider crushed under the weight of his own car, the papier-mâché artist turned into a papier-mâché figure and added to his own exhibit, the mall owner reduced to a part of his display. I'd say we're dealing with the same killer, wouldn't you? A killer eager to tell us something. But what?"

"That pride comes before the fall?" Odelia suggested.

"Possible," Chase admitted. "Teaching each of these men a lesson in humility."

We all stared as the body of this devious killer's latest victim was cut down.

"Poor guy," I said.

"And poor Odelia," said Dooley. "Now she'll never be able to get his autograph."

"I think that's the least of her worries, Dooley."

Odelia's main concern was to stop this rampaging killer before he made even more victims.

"You know what?" said Chase. "I'm sick and tired of this. It's almost as if the killer is laughing at us. I think it's time we start leveling the playing field."

"And how do you propose we do that?"

"By doing what we should have done from the start: arresting Dominic Careen."

"Did you talk to the staff?" She gestured to Jasmine Muchari and Luke Grimsby, who were standing nearby looking crestfallen.

"Yeah, I did. They didn't notice anything out of the ordinary last night. Said they didn't even realize what happened until this morning. Though Luke did see Sergio go up to the roof at some point. Sergio said he wanted to experience the storm firsthand. Ever since he was cast as Zeus he'd become fascinated with the weather, especially stormy weather."

"Figures, for a man who played the god of atmospheric phenomena. Did Luke Grimsby see anyone else go up?"

Chase shook his head. "Nope. But he said he turned in early. So if someone did join Sergio up here, he wouldn't have seen them."

"I don't understand, Chase. Sergio told us yesterday that he'd doubled his security. He had people guarding the front gate and walking the perimeter. Dogs, even."

"I spoke to the guy in charge of security, and he said that Sergio did have a visitor last night. He'd told him to keep the dogs on a leash so he did."

"So who was it?"

"He doesn't know. No one came in through the front gate, that's for sure."

"So maybe they climbed the fence?"

"Has to be. And since the dogs had been called off, they would have had access to the house. Because of the storm the patrols had been temporarily dispensed with, since it was too dangerous to walk the grounds, because of falling tree branches."

"So whoever did this must have known their way around the place, and must have been aware of the security measures Sergio had put in place."

"Looks as if Sergio knew his attacker, or told them how to get in without being seen."

"And you're thinking it must have been Dominic?"

"I don't see who else it could have been, do you?"

"But Sergio would never invite Dominic up here, would he?"

"Maybe he did. To talk things through. To find out what Dominic was up to."

They watched on as Sergio was laid out on the roof, then transferred to a stretcher. It was going to take four able-bodied men to get the actor down from there, since he was probably two hundred pounds of pure muscle—now seriously charred.

"This is a tough case, Max," said Dooley.

"Tell me about it," I murmured.

"I'm just glad that Chase and Odelia saved us from that tree last night." He shivered. "Or else we might have ended up just like Mr. Zeus over there."

It was a sobering thought, and one I didn't enjoy mulling over. "I don't think we were in any danger of being struck by lightning. More of being crushed under a falling branch."

"Or being struck by lightning, then crushed by a falling branch." He gave me a worried look. "I never realized how dangerous singing could be, Max."

"It's not the singing, Dooley. It's being out in a park during a storm."

"Not very smart of us, was it?"

"No, not very smart at all."

"I have a feeling that next time cat choir happens there won't be a lot of cats there."

I smiled. "Just you, me, Harriet and Brutus, and of course Shanille. Small but cozy."

"Maybe we could hold cat choir in the backyard."

"I doubt the neighbors would appreciate it."

"Or in church! Father Reilly wouldn't mind."

"No, but the parishioners might. It is a holy place, after all. And not everyone is convinced cats belong in church. They might think we're trespassing. God might also be offended by our caterwauling, and decide to drop the entire church on top of our heads."

Suddenly a noise alerted us of an intruder making their way to the roof. And as his head popped up from the stairwell, we saw that it was none other than Omar Wissinski. Judging from the incandescent expression on his red face, he was not a happy guy.

"I demand you arrest that man immediately!" he shouted even before he'd fully cleared the stairwell. He was waving his arms in the manner of one mimicking a windmill.

"What man would that be, Mr. Wissinski?" asked Chase.

"Careen, of course! And I demand that you do it right now, before he takes an ax to my head as well!" He gestured vaguely in the direction of the stretcher. "Or whatever he used to kill my best friend." He then seemed to realize that he was in the presence of death, and he gulped, then uttered a sort of strangled cry, and proceeded to bite down on his knuckle. "He's really dead, isn't he? Poor Sergio is dead. Struck down in his prime."

"Who told you about what happened?" asked Chase, ever the cop.

"I got a call from Luke," said Omar. "He told me to watch out." He shook his head. "He's coming for me now, isn't he? I'm the only one left. The only one left standing!" He turned a wild-eyed gaze on Chase. "Please provide me with some protection, detective. I've posted a guard in front of my shop, but I don't think that's going to stop that maniac. If anything, he'll probably mow him down, too, just to get at me!"

"I'm afraid we can't provide any police protection at this time, sir," said Chase stiffly.

"Well, you should! Can't you see I'm next? If you don't act now I'll be dead before tonight!"

"Babe, please," said Odelia softly, as she placed a hand on her husband's arm.

"I'm sorry, Mr. Wissinski, but we're doing everything we can to bring the murderer of your friends to justice."

"It's not enough, is it! Four down and one more to go—that's what that crazy person is thinking right now. It's only me that's left now!" Suddenly he was down on his knees, holding up his hands to Chase in a gesture of prayer. "Please help me, detective. Can't you see I'm desperate? Please save me from this madman. I'm begging you, please!"

"Get up, Mr. Wissinski," said Chase not unkindly as he helped the poor guy to his feet again. "I'll see what I can do, all right?"

"You'll give me police protection?"

"Yes. I'll arrange for an around-the-clock watch on your house and office."

"Thank you, sir. Thank you so much!" He nervously glanced around. "Do you think he followed me here? Do you think he's watching us now?"

"I'm sure you're quite safe here," Chase assured the man.

"He's getting paranoid, Max," said Dooley.

"Wouldn't you be? Four of his friends are dead."

"Maybe he should come and live with us? Chase can protect him much better when he's living under the same roof."

"I don't think that's such a good idea," I said.

"But why not? If he's that scared, we have to do what we can to save him."

"I'm sure that the officers Chase will pick will be more than equal to the task of keeping Mr. Wissinski safe," I said. I didn't think giving potential victims room and board was the way to go. It might set a dangerous precedent. Soon we'd be running a safe house.

At that moment, Chase had had enough of standing around, and we all repaired downstairs. I think it had finally come home to him that we needed to end this case, unless more victims would follow. And so soon we were off in his squad car. I recognized the route he was taking. He was taking us straight to the house where the Careens lived.

CHAPTER 29

We arrived just in time to catch the three Careens at home. Dominic and Rick were already standing next to their jeep when we got there, ready to take off. When they saw us driving up, blocking the driveway, father and son exchanged a look of annoyance.

"What is it now?" asked Dominic as he threw his backpack through the open window into his jeep.

"Haven't you heard?" said Chase, slamming the door of the squad car shut. "Sergio Sorbet is dead. He was killed last night."

"If you expect me to burst into tears you came to the wrong place," the bearded forester grumbled. "Good riddance is what I say."

"Is that what you told Sergio when you killed him last night?" Chase demanded.

"Here we go again," Dominic said, rolling his eyes. "How many times!"

"Where were you last night, Dominic? And you, Rick?"

"We were right here at home. Where else do you think we'd be?"

"I don't know. Out and about, maybe?"

"Did you see the weather we had last night? Being out and about was not a good idea."

"Didn't you have to be in the woods? Making sure nobody ventured out there?"

"That's not our job, detective. We make sure those woods are well kept, but it's not up to us to make sure the public stays out of them when there's a storm like the one we had."

"What about you, Rick?" asked Chase, addressing the young man. "What's your story?"

"I was here," said Rick. "We nailed some planks of wood to a window at the back, since it's a little rickety and might not have survived, and made sure not to venture out again."

"That's your story and you're sticking to it, are you?"

"It's not a story, detective. It's what happened."

Chase sighed. "So you won't mind if I ask your neighbors, will you?"

"Be my guest," said Rick.

But when I glanced over to Dominic, I saw he suddenly got a little twitchy.

Talking to the neighbors just might be a very good idea indeed.

Chase called in the assistance of some of his colleagues, and while two of his officers made sure Dominic and Rick stayed put, the others spread out and did a house-to-house to get the neighborhood's observations about the Careens' whereabouts last night.

Suddenly Chase came barging up. "Bingo," he told Odelia, who'd covered the other side of the street and now joined us in front of the house.

"What is it?" she asked.

"Turns out that Dominic did leave the house last night. Just before midnight, in fact." He strode into the house, and we all followed the long-legged detective, who now resembled a dog with a bone. Or even a man with a bone to pick—or both. "You did leave the house last night, Careen," he said loudly, as he pricked a finger in the forester's chest.

The man was pushed back and dropped down on the couch next to his wife.

Kristina looked scared, and quietly said, "Better tell him the truth, honey."

"Look, I did nothing wrong, all right?" said Dominic. "And I didn't go anywhere near Sorbet."

"So where were you?" Chase demanded.

"I went to the woods. I thought I left the door to the cabin unlocked, and wanted to make sure everything was closed up and nailed shut. We keep equipment in that cabin that's easily worth thousands of dollars, and I didn't want anything to happen to it."

"So why didn't you tell me that?"

"Because I can see which way the wind is blowing, can't I? You come barging in here, accusing us of all kinds of stuff, and I didn't want to give you any more ammunition!"

Chase stared at the man for a moment, then seemed to make up his mind. "Dominic Careen," he said, taking a pair of handcuffs from his belt, "I'm arresting you for the murder of Sergio Sorbet."

"No!" his wife cried, holding up her arms in a protective gesture.

"You can't do this," said Dominic.

"Watch me," Chase growled.

"Dad?" said Rick.

"It's all right, son," said Dominic. "We didn't do anything."

Chase read the forester his rights, and then slapped the cuffs on his wrists, escorting him out of the house, watched on by his distressed-looking wife and angry son.

"I think it's the Jonagolds that did it, Max," Dooley

commented. "A man who gets upset over missing Jonagolds is a man who's capable of anything—even murder."

"I'm not so sure, Dooley," I said. "The Jonagold incident revealed a side of Dominic that we hadn't seen yet, but that doesn't make him a murderer. Just a man who's under a lot of stress, and can be triggered by the slightest incident."

"So? The death of his daughter and his wife's illness are bigger triggers than a missing Jonagold."

"Yeah, but these murders have shown us a killer who's meticulous in both planning and execution. And that doesn't jibe with a guy who flies off the handle just because his wife's favorite apple happens to be missing from the store."

"So you don't think Dominic Careen is our killer?"

"I'm not sure," I said, as we watched Chase put Dominic into a car and officers drive off to get him booked and locked up by the strong arm of the law for safekeeping.

CHAPTER 30

While Dominic was gently stewing in the lockup—apparently a standard practice to make people more susceptible to interrogation—we decided to drop by Vince Gusta to find out more about the little black book that had found its way into Kristina Careen's possession in such a thoroughly mysterious way.

Jefferson Gusta, the original author of the notebook, may have passed away last month, but we were hoping his son might enlighten us about his father's handiwork.

The Gusta Garage was still a thriving business, or at least it looked that way when we arrived there and saw that the place was a beehive of activity. Several mechanics were hard at work trying to give broken-down cars a new lease on life, and when we entered the small office adjacent to the garage, it was Vince himself who did the honors of greeting us.

"What can I do for you?" he said, then glanced through the window to Chase's car and frowned. "Looks fine from what I can tell. Though I don't like the sound of your engine. I heard a persistent ticking noise when you drove up just now. Don't know if you noticed?"

"We're not actually here about the car," Chase said.

Vince, who was a man in his fifties with greasy coveralls, a greasy red ball cap and smudges of grease all over his face, leaned back. "Oh? Then what are you here for?"

"This," said Chase, and produced his phone, on which pictures of the black notebook were in evidence. "And this," he added, then scrolled to the page in question.

Vince took Chase's phone and stared at the evidence. "That looks like my dad's handwriting," he said as he handed the phone back. "Where did you get this?"

"It was hand-delivered to Kristina Careen two days ago," said Chase.

"Someone put it through her mail slot," Odelia clarified.

"I'm sorry, but that wasn't me," said Vince.

Chase, who'd produced his badge and now held it out to the garage owner, said, "Right now I'm not really interested in how the notebook came into Kristina Careen's possession. Were you aware that your father worked on a Mustang on October 14th thirteen years ago? He even wrote down the license plate, plus a list of the work he did on that car."

Vince, who'd darted an unhappy look at Chase's badge, shook his head. "No idea what you're talking about, detective. What my dad did or didn't do thirteen years ago is not something I'm aware of, I'm afraid."

"Were you working here at the time?"

"Oh, sure. I've been working here for as long as I can remember. All my life, in fact."

"Maybe I'll jog your memory," said Chase. "The car your dad worked on was involved in a hit-and-run accident that killed a little girl named Poppy Careen, Kristina and Dominic Careen's seven-year-old daughter. The car was registered to Dunc Hanover, and he brought it in the morning after the accident to have the bumper replaced, the front right fender fixed and repainted and generally all traces of the accident removed. Your dad did the work off the books, and never told the police and nor did Mr. Hanover."

"Is that a fact?" Vince shrugged. "My dad did a lot of dodgy stuff back in the day. But I can assure you that the way we do things now is all above board. Nothing of that sort of stuff goes on here anymore. I've made sure of that when I took over the business."

"So your dad never told you about the Careen case? Or the work he did on Hanover's Mustang?"

"Nope. Not a word. And now if you'll excuse me, I've got plenty of work to get on with."

"Did you deliver your father's notebook to the Careens?" asked Odelia.

"No, I most certainly did not. If I did, I think I'd remember."

"Do you have any idea who did?"

Vince shook his head. "No idea, sorry. Now can I get on, please?"

Chase eyed the man a little annoyedly. He didn't enjoy being given the runaround, and it was obvious we were being given the runaround now. But finally he nodded curtly, and we walked out, leaving the busy garage owner to get busy with his busy life.

But Chase wouldn't be Chase if he didn't decide to go check out the garage and poke around here and there. And since Odelia is cut from the same cloth and so are Dooley and me, we followed the cop's example. And that's how we came upon a rusty metal drum. Next to it, some ashes had fallen, and judging from the smell, there had been a recent fire.

"Looks like someone burned something here recently," I said.

"Ooh, that's right. That little black book had burn marks," said Dooley.

"Odelia!" I called out, and gestured to our human, who was just trying to peer in through a greasy window near the back of the garage. "Over here," I said.

She quickly came over, and examined the contents of the drum. "Looks like someone burned Jefferson Gusta's notebooks," she said as she dug out a half-charred leather cover, exactly the same kind of leather cover Jefferson's notebook had sported.

Chase had now also joined us, took the leather covering from Odelia, and deposited it into an evidence bag. "I'll have it checked against the notebook," he said. "Chances are it comes from the same collection."

"What do you think you're doing?" suddenly the irate voice of Vince Gusta sounded.

He was walking up to us with furious step and Chase held up the plastic baggie. "Been cleaning house, Mr. Gusta?"

"What's it to you?" the irate garage owner demanded.

"I'm investigating four murders, and if I find out that you've been burning evidence of a crime, it's got everything to do with me. And what's more, I hope you're aware that it's against the law to destroy evidence, or to lie to the police and hamper an ongoing murder inquiry. In fact I could arrest you right now and charge you with obstruction of justice."

"All right!" said the man, holding up his hands. "So I cleaned out some of my dad's old files. I didn't think there was any harm in that. He had boxes full of the stuff, and I wanted to get rid of them once and for all."

"You weren't aware that there was evidence of a crime in his notebooks? And please think carefully before you answer me this time."

Vince sighed and took off his ball cap and scratched his graying mop of hair. "I had heard of the Poppy Careen business, yes."

"Your dad told you about it?"

"He did. Said that the person responsible for the hit and run had asked him to fix up that car so it looked as good as new."

"Was he aware that he was assisting a criminal in covering up a crime?"

"At the time he had no idea that the car had been involved in the Careen girl's death. It was just another job for him. Later he found out what happened that night, and put two and two together. But of course by then it was too late. The damage was done. So he decided not to get involved and not to mention what he did to anyone."

"Except to you."

"He didn't tell me until last month. Before he died, he asked me to clean out his old files. Said there was some stuff in there that he should have gotten rid of years ago. And that's when he told me about the Careen business."

"And you didn't feel the need to tell the police?"

"I didn't want any trouble! Besides, it's been years, and I figured it was all ancient history anyway."

"You do realize that the Careens lost their daughter that night?"

"I know, yeah," he said a little sheepishly. "And I'm sorry, okay?"

"So who delivered the notebook to Kristina Careen?"

"No idea." When Chase gave him a threatening look, he added, "I swear! Someone must have picked it out of the fire and handed it to her. But it wasn't me."

Chase glanced around. "How many people knew you were burning your father's papers?"

"No one. I just decided that I better get rid of the stuff."

"Why now?"

"No reason. Just something I've been putting off since Dad died."

"It wouldn't have anything to do with the murder of Jona Morro, would it?"

The man turned a little shifty-eyed again, and I thought he probably wasn't the right person to get your car fixed. He appeared to be fundamentally dishonest.

"Mr. Gusta?" Chase insisted.

"Okay, yes! I read about the guy being killed with his own car and it reminded me of my dad's old files. So I figured I'd better get rid of them before you people started snooping around. There. Now you know the whole story. Happy?"

"Not exactly," said Chase. "In fact I'm very unhappy with you, Mr. Gusta. Not only have you repeatedly lied to me, but you have also concealed evidence of a crime, and then tried to destroy it. I think it's safe to say you'll be charged for your efforts."

"Whatever," the man muttered, then walked off, grumbling under his breath.

We were walking back to the car when a woman came hurrying out of the garage. She was also dressed in blue coveralls, and seemed eager to have speech with us.

"Not here," she said quietly when she was within speaking distance. "Meet me in the Squeaky Wheel in ten minutes. And please don't tell my husband, all right?" And before we could ask her who her husband was, she had slipped into the garage again.

Though I think it's safe to say she was probably referring to the irrepressible Vince.

CHAPTER 31

Ten minutes later we were indeed in the Squeaky Wheel, when the same woman came breezing in. She'd ditched the blue coverall and was looking more like a regular person now, in jeans and a sweater, her blond hair tied back from her wrinkle-free face. She appeared to be in her early forties. She took a seat at the table, and looked just as nervous as she had when she'd approached us back at the garage.

"I'm Mandi Gusta," she said without preamble. "And I'm the one who gave Kristina Careen that notebook."

"You're Vince's wife?" asked Chase.

She nodded, looking a little breathless. "I can't stay long, I'm sorry. If Vince found out I was talking to the police he'd be very unhappy."

"I won't waste too much of your time, then," said Chase. "What do you know about the hit and run that killed Poppy Careen?"

"Nothing. I only met Vince eight years ago."

"He never talked to you about that night? Or his dad?"

Mandi shook her head. "But I did see him burn those notebooks the other night, and I had a feeling it was important, so I fished out one notebook and discovered that it covered the month when Poppy Careen was killed. You see, I'd read in the paper about Jona Morro, and about the Careen case, and then when Vince suddenly decided to burn his dad's old papers, it just made me wonder, you know. So I decided to save that notebook from the pile, and when I saw the entry Jefferson made the day after that terrible accident, I knew that must have been the reason Vince wanted to get rid of it."

"And so you decided that Kristina should have it."

Mandi nodded. "I always wanted kids of my own, but we lost…" Her voice faltered, but she soon recovered. "We lost Jason when he was three months old. Crib death. I was heartbroken at the time, and it put a terrible strain on our marriage but we survived. So I can understand what the Careens must have been through."

"Vince obviously doesn't," said Chase, "and nor did his dad."

"Vince and Jefferson's first priority has always been the garage. The Careen tragedy got a lot of press coverage at the time, and it's never really gone away. That kind of thing puts a stain on an entire community, not just the family. And I guess Jefferson didn't want it to affect us. I think people would have blamed him for the death of that little girl. They would have blamed him for covering up a crime and protecting a murderer. And Vince desperately tried to make that threat go away, same way his dad did."

"Thanks, Mandi," said Odelia, placing a hand on the woman's arm. "It's a very brave thing you did. And I'm sure Kristina is very grateful that you decided to come forward."

"I'm not brave," said Mandi, lowering her head. "If I were brave, I'd have stood up to Vince. I wouldn't have snuck around behind his back to deliver you his dad's notebook."

"Still, it's only thanks to you that we know now who Poppy's killer was."

"And who was it?" asked Mandi.

Chase hesitated for a moment, then said, "The license plate in your father-in-law's notebook was registered to Dunc Hanover."

Mandi frowned. "The papier-mâché artist?"

Chase nodded. "Have you ever seen him in the garage?"

"No, I haven't. I didn't know he was a client."

"It's possible it was just a one-off. Maybe Dunc or one of his friends knew that Jefferson wasn't averse to doing the odd job off the books, and paid him extra to keep his mouth shut."

"Which would explain why he never said anything," Odelia added.

"I don't know about that," said Mandi, shaking her head. "Jefferson was a good person. Okay, so he accepted money under the table, but I don't think he would have knowingly helped cover up a crime. Especially if it involved the death of a little girl."

"Vince said he only found out last month, just before his dad died. Looks like Jefferson wanted to make some kind of confession."

"I don't think so," said Chase. "He gave strict instructions to have the notebooks destroyed. He was trying to protect the reputation of Gusta Garage right up until the end."

Mandi gave us a sad look. "Will you apologize to Kristina for me?" Then she frowned. "What am I saying? I'm being just as cowardly as my father-in-law was, and my husband. You know what? Don't tell her anything. I'll go over there myself and apologize in person."

"But won't you get in trouble with Vince?" asked Odelia.

"I don't care," said Mandi, straightening. "Sometimes you just have to do the right thing, and this is one of those times.

And if Vince doesn't like it, that's too bad." She got up with a smile and extended a hand. "If there's anything else, you know where to find me."

And then she walked out, not skulking around like a scared little mouse, but like a woman who knows exactly what to do and is determined to do it.

"She's a brave person," said Dooley. "To go against her husband's wishes like that."

"I think she can feel Kristina's pain," I said. "She's been through a similar experience and she knows how devastating it can be to lose a child. Even though Kristina's suffering is probably still a notch above Mandi's."

"I'm not sure, Max," said Dooley. "I think it's hard to compare suffering."

I smiled. "You're a wise cat, Dooley," I said.

"You think so?"

"Yes, I do."

"Kristina's suffering isn't over yet, is it? With her husband in prison, looks like it's only just begun."

CHAPTER 32

After spending a couple of hours in a cell at the police station, Dominic looked a lot less rugged and self-confident than usual. His face had developed a sallow complexion, and he had a sort of haunted look in his eye. The kind of look a man who's used to being out in the woods all day gets when being cooped up in a small, dingy cell.

Chase had taken a seat across from the man in the interrogation room, and Odelia and Dooley and I were watching on through the one-way mirror.

"Poor man," said Dooley, immediately taking pity on the guy. "He looks like a butterfly that's been caught."

"A big butterfly," I said.

"Or a little bird."

"Or a big bird."

The man might have been badly affected by his recent incarceration but he still looked like a lumberjack. Which is probably because he was, in effect, a lumberjack.

"So what can you tell me about last night, Dominic?" said Chase, opening proceedings.

"I was home, then I went out to check on our cabin, then I

returned home," said the other man in his customary gruff tones.

"You didn't pop over to Sergio Sorbet's place to have a chat with the man?"

"No, I did not. I don't even know where Sorbet lives."

"Lived," Chase corrected him. "He's dead now. But of course you already knew that."

"Because you told me," said Dominic, giving Chase a look of defiance.

"Four people have been killed in three days now, Dominic, and all four of them have been accused by you of having been involved in the accident that killed your daughter."

"So?"

"Do you really expect me to believe this is a coincidence?"

Dominic leaned forward. "Look, I had nothing to do with the death of these men. But if you ask me if they got exactly what they deserved, then yes, they did. And I'm not going to shed any tears over them either. They committed a crime, and they've paid for it with their lives, which is exactly as it should be."

"So you're confessing that you have something to do with what happened to them."

"All I'm confessing to is that I'm glad they're dead. And I hope they suffered just as much as my family has suffered. Though I don't think that's possible."

"I'm going to give you a chance to prove to me you're not lying," said Chase as he placed a piece of paper on the table in front of Dominic. "These are the times of death of the four victims. I want you to think carefully and write down for me where you were at these times. And don't tell me you don't remember. You're smarter than that."

Dominic glanced down at the piece of paper. "I already

told you." He tapped a stubby forefinger on the document. "Woods, woods, home, woods."

"So basically what you're saying is that your wife and son are your only alibi."

"And the trees," said the man wryly. "Don't forget about the trees."

"Very funny," said Chase grimly as he took the piece of paper and folded it.

Chase came out to take a break, and leaned against the table. "So what do you think?" he asked.

"I'm not sure," said Odelia. "Though it doesn't look good for him, does it?"

"No, it sure doesn't," Chase agreed. "And he's not putting in a lot of effort to prove he didn't do it either."

"Almost as if he doesn't care if he goes to prison or not."

They both stared at the man, who sat hunched over, staring down at the tabletop.

Just then, an officer popped her head in. "Rick Careen is here. Says he wants to see you as soon as possible."

Chase nodded curtly, and he and Odelia left the small room, followed by yours truly and Dooley, of course. We didn't want to miss a thing!

Chase didn't want to put Rick into one of the interrogation rooms, so he talked to the young man in his office instead, which was a lot less threatening or bleak.

Rick glanced around at the posters announcing that the police are your friend, and a warning that you shouldn't give pickpockets the opportunity to go through your pockets. It seemed like good advice, though of course cats don't have pockets, so we've got those nasty pickpockets fooled.

"So what did you want to talk to me about, Rick?" asked Chase.

"Is my dad still here?" asked Rick, gesturing in the general direction of the precinct.

"Your dad is helping us with our inquiries right now," said Chase gently.

"I want you to let him go," said the kid, nodding seriously.

"I'm afraid I can't do that."

"I'm here to tell you that... that it was me," said the young man.

"It was you what?" asked Chase, puzzled.

"It was me who did it," said Rick. "I killed those men. Not my dad."

"You killed them?" asked Chase, exchanging a look with Odelia.

"Yes, I did. I want to confess. So you see? You can let my dad go now. He didn't do it. I did."

"Okay, so tell me some more about that. Take me through the scene, if you will, Rick?"

"Well, first I... I killed... Jona Morro. Because he's one of the men who killed my sister."

"And how did you kill Mr. Morro?"

"I, um, I dropped a car on top of him."

"And how, exactly, did you accomplish that?"

"Easy. I'm a forester. I'm used to cutting down trees. So I simply cut down that car and dropped it on top of him."

"And Mr. Morro just lay there? He didn't fight back?"

Rick thought for a moment. "That's because I hit him first. Knocked him out?" He glanced over to Chase, to see how his words were received.

"Okay, and how about Joel Timperley? Did you kill him, too?"

"Of course. I killed all of them. All four."

"So talk me through it, Rick. What happened?"

"I, um, I walked into his office and I said I wanted to talk to him."

"When was this?"

"Um, two nights ago?"

"What time?"

"Ten, no, eleven o'clock."

"So you walked into his office, and then what?"

"Then I said I wanted him to show me the display. You know, the display for the new Zeus movie? I said I was a big fan, and I wanted him to show it to me."

"And he didn't think that was odd? That you wanted to see the display at eleven at night?"

"No, because I said I was such a big fan, see. And so we walked down, and that's when I hit him."

"You hit him."

"Yes, I knocked him out, then strung him up right next to his friend's... model."

Chase eyed the young man kindly. "Rick, I appreciate what you're trying to do, but I'm afraid it won't do your father any good."

"But I did it!" Rick cried, jumping up from his chair. "I killed them!"

"No, you didn't."

Rick sank back down, as tears sprang to his eyes.

"It's all right, Rick," said Odelia softly. "You love your dad very much, don't you?"

Rick nodded wordlessly.

"So he wasn't with you the morning Jona Morro was killed? Or Dunc Hanover?"

Rick shook his head. "I don't know where he went. He said he had some things to take care of, but he wouldn't say what. I'm afraid—I've been afraid that..."

"That he permanently took care of the men he holds responsible for your sister's death?"

Rick nodded. "He's a good man, detective. He's my hero.

And if he did... something, I know he did it because he believed it was the right thing to do."

"Rick tried to help his dad," said Dooley. "But the only thing he succeeded in doing is putting his dad in even bigger trouble than he was already in."

"Yeah, looks like Dominic's alibi just blew up in his face."

"Where was your dad when Joel was killed?" asked Chase.

"Out," said Rick.

"Just like those other times?"

"Yeah."

"And last night?"

"He said he was going to the woods to check on the cabin."

"Why didn't you go with him?"

"He didn't want me to. Said he could handle it."

"Did you notice anything out of the ordinary when he came back?"

"I don't know. By the time he returned I'd already gone to bed."

"Hasn't he said anything to you about where he was? Or to your mom?"

"Mom asked him about it, but he said it was best if she didn't know."

"That must have got you worried."

"It did." He lifted a teary face to Chase. "I think he did it, detective. I think he went out there and killed those men. And now I don't know what to do."

"What does your mom think?"

"The same. We haven't talked about it, but I can tell she thinks Dad killed them." He gulped. "He killed them all, didn't he? And now he's going to rot in prison for the rest of his life, and Mom is going to die alone—without him. And all because the police couldn't make the men who killed Poppy pay for their crime."

CHAPTER 33

Harriet and Brutus were back at the offices of Morro & Wissinski, insurance agents, and things were a little worrisome. Omar Wissinski, ever since he was conked over the head, had been behaving strangely. That morning he arrived late, and was in a real state.

"He's dead!" he cried when he finally walked in, one hour late.

"Who's dead, Mr. Wissinski?" asked Scarlett, who'd been patiently doing her nails when her boss had failed to put in an appearance.

"Sergio, of course!"

Scarlett's jaw dropped. "Zeus is dead? Oh, no!"

Omar was pacing the office, clutching at his hair for some reason, as if hoping it would provide the answers he was looking for. "She killed him. I just know she did!"

"Who killed him?" asked Scarlett, looking to the entrance just in case she needed to make a quick getaway.

Omar stopped pacing and planted himself in front of Scarlett's desk, eyeing her feverishly. "Why, the Careen woman, of course. They arrested Dominic, you know."

"Oh, that's a good thing, isn't it?" asked Scarlett, trying to get the man to calm down.

"It is good. It's very good. But it's not good enough, is it? They should arrest Kristina, too. She's behind this whole thing—I just know she is!"

"But isn't Kristina Careen agro-phobic? Or something?"

"That's what she says. But I'm sure she's faking it!"

"But she hasn't left the house in thirteen years."

"Of course she has. When no one is watching, she leaves that house—to kill my friends!"

"That's what Gran said," Harriet whispered.

"I know she did, sugar pie," said Brutus.

"She was right. Kristina Careen is faking it!"

"But if she's faking it, don't you think someone would have seen her?" asked Scarlett.

"It's easy enough to make sure you're not seen if you don't want to be," said Omar, who'd returned to pacing the floor. "You don a disguise, or you only leave the house after dark." He wheeled on Scarlett. "Which is why both Joel and Sergio were killed at night! Of course! Kristina killed Joel and Sergio, and Dominic killed Jona and Dunc and tried to kill me!" He uttered a small cry of anguish and clasped a hand to his face, eyes wide. "She's coming for me next, isn't she? Dominic is in jail, but she's still out there, biding her time." He glanced to the door, and when he saw the sturdy form of the security man standing sentinel, he seemed to lose some of his anguish. "She can't come in here, though, can she?"

"No, sir," said Scarlett. "You're perfectly safe in here. Kristina can't get to you."

"I need security at the house, too," Omar mumbled, fingering his lips. "I'll have to up security at the house, at the office… for as long as Kristina is still out there. That cop said he was going to provide police protection but so far I haven't seen it."

"And what about the son?" asked Scarlett the logical question.

"What about the son?" asked Omar, his head jerking up and his feverish gaze returning to Scarlett.

"Well, if the mother is involved, and so is the father, don't you think the son might be involved, too?"

Omar's jaw had dropped as he considered this possibility. "Oh, God. He's going to take over his parents' mission, isn't he? You see it in movies all the time. James Bond kills the father and then twenty years later the son suddenly pops up and tries to kill James!"

"Maybe you should tell the police," Scarlett suggested helpfully.

"Oh, the police are absolutely useless!" Omar cried viciously. "They simply twiddle their thumbs and do nothing while all four of my friends are being butchered by these maniacs!" He directed a wrathful look at the ceiling, as if it had personally insulted him, and muttered, "I'll just have to take care of this myself, won't I? I'll have to handle this personally, if the police aren't going to." He nodded to himself. "Yes, that's what I'll do."

"I wouldn't do that, if you were you, sir," said Scarlett, holding up her hand to draw her employer's attention.

"Oh, who asked you!" the man spat, then retreated into his office and slammed the door.

"Uh-oh," said Scarlett as she took out her phone. "We better warn… someone," she said to no one in particular, then placed the phone to her ear. Moments later it connected. "Vesta? I think Omar is about to do something bad to the Careens. Yeah, he's gone a little nuts."

"Or completely nuts," said Harriet.

"Can you blame him?" said Brutus. "His four best friends have been killed. And he believes the killer is going to come for him now. I don't blame the guy for losing it."

"Well, he better keep it together until Chase has solved the crime," said Harriet.

"Chase!" Brutus cried. "You mean Max."

"You think Max will be able to figure out who's responsible for these murders?"

"Of course he will. Max is a smart cookie. If anyone can figure it out, it's him."

Harriet smiled at her mate. "He is very clever, isn't he?"

"Of course he is. But don't tell him I said that. He'll get cocky."

"Your secret is safe with me, boogie bear."

"Though I think we better tell him to get a move on, before Omar puts out a contract on Kristina and Rick Careen."

"You don't think…"

Brutus cocked a serious whisker. "I bet he's in there going through the yellow pages right now, looking for killers for hire to take out Kristina and her son."

"What a mess."

Scarlett had finished her phone call, and hiked her purse higher up her shoulder. "Let's go, you guys," she said. "We're meeting M. Or is it Q? I've never seen a James Bond movie, can you believe it?"

"Too bad she doesn't understand a word we say," said Harriet. "Because I have a feeling Scarlett and I would get along like gangbusters."

They walked past the security man, and Scarlett told the guy to keep a close eye on Mr. Wissinski, and make sure he didn't do anything stupid. The man eyed her curiously. "It's not my job to make sure he doesn't do anything stupid, ma'am," he said. "It's my job to make sure nobody does anything stupid to him." And having said what he had to say, he resumed his wide-legged stance and adopted a thousand-yard stare.

They all hurried to the food court where they found Gran, and within minutes Scarlett had delivered her report and so had Harriet and Brutus.

"That doesn't sound good," said Gran, and her face took on a serious note as she took out her own phone and called Odelia to deliver an urgent message that Omar might pose a clear and present danger to the Careens—or at least those Careens who hadn't been arrested yet. As it was, it now looked as if Dominic was in the best position of all. At least Omar or the hitman he was about to employ presumably couldn't get at him.

"What did she say?" asked Scarlett.

"She said she'll handle it," said Gran, looking grim-faced. She patted Harriet and Brutus on the head. "You did good," she said, then absentmindedly patted Scarlett on the head, too, as if she was part of the feline contingent.

Scarlett eyed her friend strangely. "Are you all right, Vesta?"

"Ever since this assignment started I've drunk way too much hot chocolate," said Gran. "Next time I'll stick to chamomile tea instead."

CHAPTER 34

Chase had sent Rick home, and as he and Odelia discussed the phone call from Gran, announcing that Omar was going a little nuts and was thinking about taking matters into his own hands, a police officer stuck her head in and said that Justina McMenamy was waiting and had asked to talk to Chase.

"Send her in," said Chase, and frowned to his wife. "Did you ask her to drop by?"

"No, I didn't," said Odelia.

"Well, let's hear what she has to say."

Dunc's fiancée looked a lot better than the last time we'd seen her. But then of course she'd just had a terrible shock then. She seemed to have recovered a little, though the fact that she was dressed in black from head to toe told us she was still in mourning.

"You wanted to see me?" asked Chase.

"Yes," said Justina, taking a seat next to Odelia. "I got a call from Kristina Careen this morning."

Chase arched an eyebrow in surprise. "Kristina called you?"

"Yeah, she said that she knew that Dunc was the person who killed her daughter that fateful night. She said he took his car in for repairs the morning after the accident, so now she's got evidence that he was her daughter's murderer. She said she's going to bring charges against Dunc—belatedly, of course—and thought I should know."

"Okay," said Chase, sitting back and tapping a pencil against his desk.

"The thing is," said Justina, "that it wasn't Dunc who was driving that Mustang."

"It wasn't?"

"No. I'm going to tell you what I just told Kristina. The boys used to swap cars all the time. And I know for a fact that it wasn't Dunc who was behind the wheel of that car."

"Is this what he told you?"

"It is."

"Why didn't you tell us this before?" asked Chase. "You said you'd never heard of the Careen case before. That Dunc had never mentioned any of this to you! You lied to us!"

Justina looked away. "I-I wanted to protect Dunc's legacy. Make sure that his name and his reputation aren't sullied. But now that Kristina is threatening to sue…" She shrugged.

"So who was the person who drove your fiancé's car that night?"

"I don't know. He wouldn't tell me. You see, he was very loyal to his friends, even though lately they hadn't been seeing as much of each other as they used to. In fact he only told me about this when I asked him. I read an article in the paper. Commemorating ten years of Poppy Careen's death. So I asked him about it, since the article mentioned him and the others. He swore up and down that it wasn't him. Said someone else was driving his car that night, and he had nothing to do with what happened."

"But he wouldn't say who did."

Justina shook her head. "They were all pretty reckless, you know. Used to be into all kinds of stuff. Poker games where they played for high stakes. One of them once lost a house, and another one a boat. He told me some crazy stories. But Dunc wasn't like the others. He couldn't afford to lose a house or a boat. He wasn't rich like them. So he was always different. More careful. And ever since we met, he started distancing himself from his friends even more. Said he regretted some of the stuff they got up to back in the day."

"So what happened to Dunc's Mustang?" asked Chase.

"I don't know. All I know is that he didn't have it anymore."

"He didn't say where it ended up?"

"No. All I know is that he got rid of it at some point."

"Dumped it in a lake, maybe? Or the junkyard?"

"He never said. And I'm afraid I never asked, either."

Chase studied her for a moment. "Have you told us the truth this time, Justina?"

She looked up. "Yes, I have, detective—I swear."

After Justina had left, Chase looked thoughtful. "So if Dunc didn't drive his Mustang that night, who did?"

"There's only one person left who can tell us," said Odelia.

Chase nodded. "Omar Wissinski." He grabbed his jacket. "I think we better have a chat with our Mr. Wissinski."

"What about Dominic?"

"Oh, he can think about his sins some more."

Moments later, we were in Chase's car, driving back to the Keystone Mall—though very soon now it would probably change its name to Timpermall Hampton Keys. At least if the standoff between the Hampton Keys mayor and the Timperleys was resolved.

The security guard planted in front of Omar Wissinski's office stepped aside when Chase showed him his credentials and even opened the door for us.

"If this guy keeps standing there," I said, "business will become very slow for Omar."

"Why?" asked Dooley. "Don't you think people will like knowing they're safe inside?"

"I doubt it, Dooley. This isn't a jewelry store or a bank. It's just an insurance agency. People will start to think that Omar is up to something funny with their money."

"Like investing it in a bitcoin scheme, you mean?"

I smiled. "Something like that."

Omar looked a little harried when we stepped into his office. Or I should probably say even more harried than the last time we saw him, on the roof of his friend Sergio's house.

"I'm so glad you're here," he said, shifting nervously in his seat. "I called the station but they said you were busy. And yet here you are. Quick work, detective. And I appreciate it! So I want you to arrest Kristina Careen and her son Rick. I know that Kristina has you all fooled into thinking she's arachnophobic."

"Agoraphobic," Odelia corrected him.

"Whatever. But that's just a ruse, see? She's been coming and going without anyone noticing, and murdering my friends! As I see it, she killed Joel and Dunc, while Dominic killed Jona and Sergio and tried to kill me. And their son Rick is assisting them both!"

"And you have proof of this, sir?" asked Chase.

Omar's face fell. "Proof! I don't need proof. Isn't it obvious? The woman is dangerous! There's a reason we all took out a restraining order against her and her family. But that hasn't stopped her. Oh, no. On the contrary. She's on a rampage. A murder spree!"

"We're actually not here about that," said Chase, holding up his hand to stem the flow of words.

"You're not?" asked Omar, his face expressing his surprise.

"We talked to Dunc's fiancée, and she told us that Dunc didn't drive his Mustang that night—the car that was implicated in the hit and run that killed Poppy Careen."

"He didn't?"

"No. Dunc said you swapped cars, and someone else was driving his Mustang."

Omar was silent for a moment, as he stared at Chase and Odelia, who were clearly expecting an answer. The insurance man licked his lips nervously.

"So who was it, Omar?" asked Chase. "Who was driving Dunc's car?"

Omar finally relented. "Okay, so we were street racing that night."

"In the Careens' neighborhood?"

"Yes. The reason we didn't tell you is obvious, I think. But now that he's gone…"

"Who was it, Omar? Who was behind the wheel?"

Omar heaved a deep sigh and seemed to deflate like a balloon. "Sergio," he said quietly. "We all swore an oath never to tell. A pact, you know. All for one and one for all and all that. We knew it could have been either one of us who'd gotten into that fatal accident, so we decided to close ranks. If anyone had found out that Sergio was behind the wheel of that car, his life would have been over. He never would have had the career he had."

"Who came up with the idea to take the car to Jefferson Gusta?"

"Joel. His dad was a regular customer of the Gusta

Garage, and he knew that Gusta wouldn't mind accepting some money under the table in exchange for a rush job. He also knew that Gusta wouldn't talk. Joel's dad had been in a minor accident and when he took his car to Gusta things had been handled discreetly, so Joel knew he could trust Gusta."

"So he fixed up Dunc's Mustang?"

"Yeah, and Joel paid him a large sum of money to make sure he kept his mouth shut."

"What happened to the Mustang?"

"Dunc drove around with it for another couple of years, until it broke down and Gusta agreed to take it to a wrecker. It probably got demolished, the parts sold as scrap."

"So the car is gone, huh?"

"Yeah, unless Gusta kept it, but I don't think he did. He was as good as his word."

Chase nodded. "You should have told us sooner, Omar," he said. "If you had, your friends might still be alive now."

"I know," said Omar, a haunted look in his eyes. "But I couldn't."

"Yeah, I know. The bachelor pact." He got up. "You're not going to do anything stupid about Kristina and her son, are you, Omar?"

"I don't know what you mean," said Omar.

"I think you do." He fixed the man with a serious look, and finally Omar looked away. "Cause if anything happens to that woman or to Rick, I'll know where to find you."

And with these words, we left the office.

CHAPTER 35

Odelia had dropped us in town, and since I was feeling a little peckish, I decided it was high time we paid a visit to Kingman again. Also, I was completely stuck, with the case not moving the way I wanted it to move. And for some reason a visit to Kingman often manages to get me unstuck. I don't know what it is about that voluminous cat, but he seems to spread these nuggets of wisdom, even if he's fully unaware of it, that never fail to point me in the right direction.

"Hiya, fellas," he said as we walked up. He gestured to a full bowl of a sort of greenish-brownish kibble. "Taste it at your own peril," he said. "And don't say I didn't warn you."

"What is it?" asked Dooley as he gave it a sniff.

"I'm not sure. Some Russian fella dropped it off this morning, and said the stuff is very popular with their Russian cats. I think he mentioned peas and spinach?"

I wrinkled up my nose. "I don't like peas or spinach," I said.

"Who does?"

"Have you tried it?"

"One nugget. I upchucked it the moment it went down." He pointed to a sad-looking lonely piece of kibble on the sidewalk, that indeed looked as if it had been in someone's stomach recently.

So I kindly declined to sample this Russian kibble, and lay down next to my friend.

"How is the case going?"

"Don't ask," I said. "We've got one guy in jail right now, who refuses to tell us where he's been, and it looks as if he's the one behind the whole thing."

He looked over to me. "But you're not fully convinced, are you?"

"Not really. I mean, why wait thirteen years to start murdering the men you think are responsible for your daughter's death?"

"Didn't you mention that the wife doesn't have much longer to live?"

"Yeah, but even so."

We were both silent, and suddenly the sounds of munching reached my ears. When I looked over, I saw that Dooley was digging into the Russian kibble, and already half of the bowl's contents had been transferred to his stomach. He looked up when he felt us looking at him. "It's pretty good," he announced. "Tastes a little funny, but not so bad."

"Be careful, Dooley," I said. "That you don't get sick."

"That's all right. I think I'd know if it was bad for me."

I wasn't as convinced as he was. "So how about you?" I asked. Kingman looked a little subdued, I thought. "Still recovering from that storm last night?"

"Oh, no, I'm fine," he said. "So I got soaked to the skin. And so I had to be saved from that tree. And so the fireman who rescued me said he'd never seen a fatter cat in his life."

"He said that?"

Kingman nodded. "Maybe that spinach would do me

good," he said, eyeing the green kibble dubiously. "I am a big cat, Max. Maybe I'm too big?"

"Nonsense," I said. "As long as Vena gives you a clean bill of health, you're good."

"Yeah, but if even a fireman figures I'm too big…"

"Look, you're just like me," I said, not taking any of this nonsense. "You've got big bones, that's all."

"I guess," he said, then placed his head on his paws and smiled. "Wilbur finally managed to get hold of his brother last night."

"About selling him part of the store?"

"Yeah. Turns out Rudolph is in Germany, and having a ball. I didn't know Germans were so crazy about thrash metal. Though Rudolph said it's actually death metal."

"Death metal!" Dooley cried. "That sounds horrible!"

"It doesn't actually involve dead people," Kingman assured us. "It's just a name."

"So he's drawing big crowds, is he?"

"Not really. As far as we can tell from the band's Facebook page they're still mostly playing small venues, and when Wilbur suggested he buy part of Rudolph's share, he sounded happy, so I think he needs the money."

"So Wilbur might be able to save the store from the clutches of the Timperleys?"

"Yeah, looks like it. Rudolph has agreed to give him another ten-percent share in exchange for some ready cash now, and the rest paid in installments over the next couple of years or so, and Wilbur has already wired him the money. So it looks like a done deal."

"Hey, but that's great, Kingman. So you and Wilbur will be able to stay here."

"I know," said Kingman, continuing to look subdued. "It's just sad, you know, this sibling rivalry. Wilbur and Rudolph always seem to want to one-up each other. Always in competition. Rudolph actually tried to convince Wilbur he was playing one of Germany's biggest venues, and that the place was sold out. Even though we could see from the band's Facebook page that they played for five guys and a dog in some basement in Düsseldorf."

"Rudolph wants to make it look as if he's a big success."

"Yeah, and he said he only sold his share in the store because he cares about Wilbur so much, even though it's obvious he simply needs the money." He shrugged. "It's good for us, though. At least we'll be able to hang onto the store and the apartment."

I thought about what Kingman said, and suddenly there was a slight whirring sensation in that big noggin of mine, as several pieces of the puzzle seemed to fall into place. "Thanks, Kingman," I said. "You've helped me more than you know."

"You're very welcome, buddy."

Dooley came over, and for some reason his face looked as green as the kibble he'd just eaten. "I don't feel so good," he confessed, and suddenly and without warning upchucked everything he'd just eaten. "Sorry about that," he muttered, looking miserable.

"Are you all right?" I asked, as I placed a solicitous paw on his back.

"More or less," he said.

Wilbur, who'd noticed our friend's incident, now came out of the store with a brush, and proceeded to sweep the contents of Dooley's stomach into the gutter. "Thanks for that, Dooley," he said. "At least now I know not to buy that Russian junk anymore." And he returned into his store, whistling a pleasant tune.

"Looks like we're Wilbur's guinea pigs," I said.

"Of course we are," said Kingman. "I thought you knew!"

"I feel sick, Max," said Dooley weakly. "Can we go home now?"

"Yes, Dooley," I said. "But first we need to drop by Odelia's office." I gave him a look of determination. "There's something I have to take care of before we go."

CHAPTER 36

Scarlett gently knocked on the door of her employer's office and listened for his telltale 'Come!' It took a while before it came this time, but when it finally did, she opened the door and said, "I have a customer who would very much like to see you, Mr. Wissinski. She's a personal friend of mine, and I have told her you can see her now." She lowered her voice and added, "She's also very, very rich!"

"Oh, all right," said Omar resignedly. After Chase and Odelia's visit he hadn't stepped out of the office once, and now looked even more dejected than before. "Send her in."

Harriet and Brutus exchanged a look of excitement when Gran stepped into Omar's office. She had brought a suitcase with her, and shlepped it in as she took a seat.

"Leave the door open, will you?" said Omar. "Air this place out a little."

"Do you think he'll take Gran on as a client?" asked Brutus.

"I'm sure he will," said Harriet. "She is, after all, exactly the kind of client Omar likes."

They watched on as Scarlett returned to her desk, and Gran took a seat in front of the insurance man.

"What can I do for you?" asked Omar, steepling his fingers and offering Gran his most ingratiating smile.

"Well, the problem is that I have all of this money, Mr. Omar," said Gran. "And now I don't know what to do with it, you see."

Omar's brow quivered. "Tell me more."

"Well, my husband died a couple of months ago, and he left me a very large fortune. Unfortunately he made most of it by buying and selling illegal goods."

"Your husband was in the import-export business?"

"Something like that," said Gran. She leaned in. "My husband was a drug dealer."

Omar looked surprised. "A drug dealer!"

"Yes, please don't tell anyone. Scarlett, who's my best friend, told me that you're very discreet. And I hope I can count on your discretion now."

"Oh, but of course, my dear lady. So how much money are we talking about here?"

"Well, I've always known that Bruce kept his money hidden in the basement. He liked suitcases, you see. The sturdy kind. And he kept on buying new ones online all the time. So after he died, I went down there and found about a dozen suitcases. I opened one and there was a hundred grand in there, all in small notes."

"A hundred thousand dollars!"

"They looked messy and some of them had blood on them, and some looked as if they'd been jammed in some guy's underpants, but hey—money doesn't stink, right?"

"It certainly doesn't."

"And since there are eleven more suitcases in my basement, I think you can see how that puts me in a spot."

"Oh, I think I do."

"I've heard a lot of good things about bitcoin. About how it's super-safe, and the taxman hasn't got a clue that you even have it, nor do the boys in blue."

"Bitcoin works with a digital wallet that's locked with a digital key, and only the person with the key can open the wallet. So it is indeed very safe and very, shall we say, discreet." He smiled an unctuous smile at Gran. "So how much money were you thinking of transferring into bitcoin, Mrs…"

"Moll. Mary Moll. Well, all of it, of course. Though maybe I should keep one suitcase for everyday expenses. Like my housekeeper and my shopping."

"I'm honored that you would think of me to take care of this little problem for you," said Omar.

"Scarlett said you were the man to see. I thought of taking everything to my bank, but she said that wasn't a good idea."

"Banks have an obligation to report any money deposited into an account over a certain amount. If you were to take your husband's suitcases into a branch of your bank it would raise all kinds of red flags, and the police would be all over you in a matter of minutes."

"But you won't tell them, right? After all, my dear Bruce earned that money fair and square. It's not his fault that the government thinks crystal meth shouldn't be allowed. I mean, all he did was supply a product and fulfill a need. In fact the man was a saint."

"Absolutely," said Omar severely. "So when were you thinking about making your… investment?"

"I brought one suitcase with me," said Gran, and hefted the suitcase onto Omar's desk. It was big and bulky and the insurance man eyed it eagerly.

"Well, let's open her up, shall we?" he suggested.

Gran adjusted the dials for the security locks and popped the clasps. Omar unzipped the monstrosity and stood eyeing the contents of the suitcase with eyes glimmering with excitement. "Now will you look at that," he murmured, rubbing his hands with glee.

"He looks like a man who's just found treasure," said Brutus.

"He does indeed," said Harriet.

"Do you think you'll be able to handle such a big investment?" asked Gran.

"Oh, absolutely," said Omar. "The Morro & Wissinski bitcoin fund is exactly the thing you need, Mrs. Moll. And in fact if you'd like me to fetch your other suitcases for you, I'd be more than happy to drop by this evening and pick them up."

"Let's first make this deposit," said Gran, "and see how it goes."

"Of course. I'll start on the paperwork, shall I? And in the meantime here's a brochure explaining the ins and outs of our bitcoin fund."

And as he handed Gran a glossy brochure, he started filling out the paperwork for the transfer of a hundred thousand dollars in drug money to the Morro & Wissinski bitcoin fund.

"Looks like he took the bait," said Harriet happily.

"Now let's hope he takes it all the way," said Brutus.

CHAPTER 37

That night we were staking out Omar Wissinski's place, and frankly I was feeling a little crowded. There were four humans in the car, and four cats, and even though Chase's squad car is roomy, it isn't as roomy as all that.

"You really should buy yourself a bigger car, Chase," said Gran as she shuffled about uncomfortably. "Especially now with the baby coming, you're going to want to get a family car. A nice big Volvo."

Chase directed a look of distaste at her through the rearview mirror. "Never in my life am I going to buy a Volvo."

"Why not?" asked Gran. "I like Volvo. Big and spacious, and very, very safe."

"They do get good reviews, babe," said Odelia.

"I don't care. I'm not buying a Volvo."

"And why is that?" asked Scarlett.

"Because I don't want to be the laughingstock of the precinct, that's why!"

"Only idiots would laugh at a man who drives a Volvo,"

said Gran. "Besides, what's more important: the opinion of your colleagues, or the safety of your family?"

"Well, if you put it that way…" Chase grumbled.

"I think a Volvo station wagon is the way to go," said Scarlett. "And a bright color, so it stands out in traffic. It's much safer that way, you know. Better than gray or dark blue."

"So a bright yellow Volvo station wagon it is," said Gran.

"God, no," said Chase, much to the others' amusement.

"Why do babies need big cars?" asked Dooley. "I thought they were small?"

"Babies are small to begin with," said Harriet. "But they grow very quickly."

"And also, nobody stops with one baby," said Brutus. "Soon there's two, then three, and before you know it, there are four or five or six."

"Six babies!" Dooley cried. "But there's no space in the house for six kids!"

"Brutus is just kidding," I said. "I don't think Odelia and Chase are ready for six kids."

"Let's start with just the one," said Odelia, who'd overheard our conversation.

"So when is the baby arriving, exactly?" asked Dooley nervously.

"Nine months," I said. "Though now it's probably a little less than nine months."

"Nine months," Dooley murmured. "That's still a long time, isn't it, Max?"

"Oh, absolutely. Nine months is like an eternity. Plenty of time for you to get ready."

"Ready? Why do I have to get ready?" he asked in panicky tones. "Is something terrible going to happen when that baby arrives? Are we going to get kicked out of the house!"

"No, of course not!" said Harriet. "What Max means to

say is that you have to get ready psychologically. Get used to the idea of a third person living in the same house with us."

"A very tiny person," said Brutus. "So tiny you'll hardly notice it."

"Oh, we will notice it," said Harriet. "Babies might be small, but they take up a lot of space—figuratively speaking. For one thing, they're very, very loud."

"Some babies are loud," I said. "Others are very, very quiet."

"Let's hope we get a quiet baby," said Dooley. He thought for a moment. "If it's loud, can we return it and get a quiet one instead?"

"I'm afraid not, Dooley," I said. "You can't return a baby once you have it."

"Too bad," said my friend. "There should be a return policy for babies."

"Now wouldn't that be a thing," said Gran with a sigh. I had the impression she would have returned her son if she'd had the opportunity.

"Quiet, you guys," said Scarlett. "Look, there's movement."

There was definitely movement across the street. Omar, who'd arrived in his own car, a Toyota Corolla, now appeared at the door, looked left and right, then hurried over to his car, drove it into his garage, and quickly closed the garage door again.

"Showtime," Chase grunted, and got out of the car.

"Let's go!" said Gran excitedly.

"No, you stay here," said Chase, and made to close the door.

"Are you kidding me? I'm going," said Gran.

"It's not safe, Vesta," said the stalwart cop.

"It's my money!"

"It's not your money, Gran," said Odelia.

"Oh, but it is. Or at least Bruce's money. The money he made selling crystal meth."

"There is no Bruce!" Scarlett reminded Gran. "It's just a ruse, Vesta!"

"I don't care. It's my money, and I'm not letting it out of my sight."

"Oh, all right," said Chase. "But you keep out of sight, will you?"

"I'm going to be invisible," said Gran, ducking down low as she exited the vehicle.

Scarlett and Odelia now made out to exit the car.

"You two better stay put," said Chase.

"I'm coming," Scarlett stated decidedly.

"Too right you are," said Gran. "We're the neighborhood watch, after all."

"Best you stay here," said Chase, addressing his wife. "With the baby…"

"Are you kidding me?" said Odelia. "I'm not staying in the car."

"But…"

"Is this how it's going to be from now on? Cause if it is, I'll tell you right now, mister, that you're very much mistaken!"

"Oh, fine!" said Chase, and held the door open for his lady love, then helped her out as if she was an invalid. Odelia slapped his hand away, and Chase gave her a nice eyeroll.

Before he could close the door, however, four cats also walked out, causing the big cop to groan in dismay. "This isn't a sting operation," he lamented. "This is a family trip!"

"Which is why you need a Volvo!" said Scarlett cheerfully.

"Or a minivan," Gran added mischievously.

"I am *not* getting a minivan," said Chase through gritted teeth.

"Of course you aren't," said Gran, patting him on the back. "You're getting a Volvo."

We all stalked across the street, then circled the house and soon found ourselves in Omar Wissinski's backyard, where we all distributed ourselves amongst the available shrubs, and hunkered down to see what the guy was up to with Gran's drug money. Though as Odelia had pointed out, it wasn't Gran's money, of course. In fact it was Uncle Alec's money—or rather money the police had recently confiscated from a drug dealer.

We didn't have long to wait, for soon Omar opened the glass sliding door and came out, carrying Gran's suitcase as he did. He glanced left, he glanced right, then ventured into the backyard, and as he reached the halfway point between his porch and the end of the yard, he crouched down and seemed to reach into the ground. We heard a sort of clanking sound, and suddenly the grass seemed to tilt up at an angle!

It was some kind of hatch he'd pulled, and moments later the man disappeared into the opening, walking down a staircase, and was soon gone from view. Two arms reached up, took a firm hold of the suitcase and then dragged it down with him and it was gone.

"Bruce's money!" Gran hissed. "He's taking it to China!"

"I'm afraid to ask, but why China?" Chase hissed back.

"Well, it's the other side of the world, isn't it?"

"I don't think that tunnel leads all the way to China, Gran," said Odelia.

"Okay, so Mexico, then. It probably leads him straight across the border."

"We're thousands of miles from the border!" Scarlett cried.

"Shush!" Chase whispered. "Can you please be quiet—all of you!"

"I think he's probably going to Australia," said Dooley. "Not China."

"You may have a point, buddy," I said, in a good mood now that my hunch had panned out.

It took about five or ten minutes before Omar finally returned, and Gran was getting anxious as time stretched on. "He's gone to China, I'm telling you!"

"Australia!" Dooley countered.

"He's just counting the money, that's all," said Chase.

Finally the man resurfaced, and Chase got up out of his crouch.

"Hello, Mr. Wissinski," he said, walking up to the insurance agent. "Out for a stroll, are we?"

Omar gulped as he stared up at the cop, who stood towering over him.

"I-I-I," he stuttered as he now hurriedly crawled up and made to close the hatch.

But Chase beat him to it. "Not so fast," he said, and held the hatch open with one hand while he took hold of Omar's wrist with the other, applying a viselike grip to the man's appendage. "Let's see what we have here." He turned to Odelia, who had joined him. "Take a look, will you, Mrs. Kingsley?"

"By all means, Mr. Kingsley," said Odelia, and lightly descended down an aluminum ladder into the depths. Dooley and I had also walked up, followed by Harriet and Brutus, and stared down to see what Odelia would find.

"Got it!" finally our human shouted, and soon returned, a big grin on her face. "It's all there," she announced.

"You can't do this," Omar protested feebly. "This is my private property!"

"No, this is my private property!" said Gran, also walking onto the scene.

Omar goggled at her.

189

"Mr. Wissinski, meet my grandmother Vesta Muffin," said Odelia.

"Your-your grandmother?" asked the insurance man.

"And my best friend," said Scarlett, the last person to pop out of those bushes. "I hadn't lied about that."

"But I had lied about the money," said Gran. "And I didn't have a husband named Bruce. I had a husband, but his name was Jack and he was a philanderer, not a drug dealer."

"The money my grandmother gave you was a loan from the police department," Odelia explained.

"Yeah, it was drug money, all right," said Chase, "but it doesn't belong to Vesta."

"Unfortunately," Gran added under her breath.

"So you took the money your clients gave you and stashed it in your private underground safe, did you?"

Omar stared from the cop to Odelia to Scarlett to Gran, then finally said, "Okay, fine."

"There is no Morro & Wissinski bitcoin fund, is there?" asked Odelia.

Omar shook his head. "No, there isn't."

"It's just a scam to collect money to pay off your gambling debts."

"Yeah, I guess you got my number."

"When did Jona find out?" asked Chase.

"Last week. The guy I owed money to called the office, and Jona picked up. It didn't take him long to put two and two together."

"So he had to die, didn't he?"

Omar nodded morosely. "I didn't want to kill him, but he was threatening to expose everything and kick me out of the company. I would have been ruined. I tried to reason with him, but he said he'd been patient enough with me and I'd had my last chance and blown it."

"This had happened before?"

"Yeah, I'd gambled and lost before, and Jona and the others had made up for the money I lost. But this time he said enough was enough. No more handouts. I was on my own."

"He told the others?"

"He did. They all knew what happened, and they all decided that it was time for me to pay the piper. But I couldn't, could I? I owe over half a mil. I'll never be able to pay them back. They'll kill me, just to set an example. Jona and the others were supposed to be my best friends. But instead they handed me a death sentence."

"So instead you decided that they all had to die, so you could live."

"That's exactly how it was. Especially Dunc was pretty damning in his opinion. He was the one who decided to betray the pact by getting hitched to that stupid broad." He frowned. "Who was he to get all high and mighty all of a sudden?"

"So they all had to go."

"But how were you going to repay your debt?" asked Gran.

"Easy. I'd been taking money from gullible old ladies like yourself for weeks, behind Jona's back, of course, and putting the money down here until I had enough. Only Jona found out when Mrs. Stooge dropped by and wanted her money back. Jona was furious."

"One more reason for him to die."

"If I got rid of him, his half of the business would revert to me, and if I could get a few more payments, I'd be able to repay my debt and be home free. The rest of the money I was going to use to get out of here."

"So you were going to fleece your customers and skip out?" asked Chase.

"Sure! Nothing to keep me here."

"And to make sure no one would come looking for you, you decided to frame the Careens."

"They had it coming," he said with a shrug. "Hounding us about that stupid accident for years. I thought I could kill two birds with one stone. Pay off my debt, get rid of the Careens, and make sure I was set up for life, with enough money to retire on."

"My Bruce's money!" Gran cried.

"Gran, there is no Bruce," Odelia reminded her.

"Oh, right."

"So is that why you killed your friends in such an ostentatious way?" asked Chase. "To make sure the police would think the Careens were behind the murders?"

"Oh, absolutely. The car on top of Jona, Joel's living statue —or dead statue—Dunc's papier-mâché display, Sergio's death by lightning. All to point the finger at the Careens. And it worked, didn't it? You thought Dominic was behind the whole thing from the start."

"I did," Chase confessed. "Though I never felt absolutely convinced."

"And why is that?"

"Mainly because you didn't die, I guess. I mean, here we had four vicious murders, all carried out meticulously, and the only one who'd walked away was you, with only a light concussion. That didn't sit right with me from the start."

Omar shrugged. "I could have hit myself harder but I hate pain."

Chase nodded curtly. "Omar Wissinski, you're under arrest for the murders of Jona Morro, Dunc Hanover, Joel Timperley and Sergio Sorbet."

Omar winced, then said, softly, "And you can add Poppy Careen."

We all stared at the man.

"You did that?" said Odelia, shocked.

Omar nodded. "Yup. One more reason for the others to turn their back on me." He shrugged. "Guess they figured I'd caused them enough trouble over the years." He grinned a sad grin. "It used to be one for all and all for one, but lately it was all against one, instead. I guess even friendship has its limits. And I reached that limit a long time ago."

CHAPTER 38

"Omar was in real trouble," I said as I leisurely picked at a piece of sausage Odelia had placed within paw's reach. "Not only was he in debt because of his gambling addiction, but his business partner was trying to get him kicked out of the company, his friends no longer took his calls, and his dad had changed his will to make sure his inheritance would go to Omar's younger brother Argyle and not to him."

"So that's what the argument between Omar and his mom was about," said Harriet.

She was lying next to me on the porch swing, and so were Dooley and Brutus. From our perch we had a perfect view of the backyard, where a family party was in full swing.

"Yeah, Omar didn't think it was fair that Argyle would inherit and he would be cut out of his parents' will, but Garth and Julia Wissinski knew about their oldest son's gambling addiction, and didn't want one cent to go to him in the event of their death. Also, Omar was afraid that the pact was breaking down, and that his friends were prepared to tell the truth about what happened thirteen years ago on that residential street."

"Omar was driving Dunc's Mustang that night, wasn't he?" said Harriet.

"Yes, he was. And until now he'd been able to rely on the bachelor pact, but one by one his friends had started distancing themselves from him, and he felt that they could turn their back on him any moment and go to the cops to finally turn him in."

"So that's why he killed his best friends," said Brutus, shaking his head. "What a guy."

"I would never turn my back on my friends," said Dooley earnestly. "Or kill them."

"I know you wouldn't, Dooley," I said. "But Omar felt he didn't have a choice. He was in a tight place financially, with a huge gambling debt hanging over him, and he thought that if he didn't move against his friends, they'd move against him, and his life would be over."

We watched on as Scarlett showed a shiny brochure of a yellow Volvo station wagon to Chase, who eyed it with marked distaste. "And look at all that space!" she said, extolling the virtues of the car. "And it's got the best safety record."

"What I don't understand," said Harriet, "is why Dominic refused to tell the truth about where he was at the time of the murders. He was only making things harder for himself."

"Dominic and Kristina had started going through an experimental treatment for her cancer. A clinic in Hampton Keys that has seen some remarkable results. But since they hadn't told Rick about the cancer, they couldn't very well come out with the truth."

"They didn't want their son to know about his mom's cancer?"

"They were going to wait. They hoped they'd be able to fight the cancer, and make it go into remission, and then Rick would never have to find out. They felt that their son had already been through enough with the death of his sister, and didn't want him to think his mom was going to die, too. So they decided to keep her disease a secret for as long as they could."

"But I thought Kristina was afraid to leave the house?" said Dooley.

"She was, but when she got sick, she had no choice. So with the help of her therapist, she gradually overcame the phobia, even though she still has a hard time with it, even now. Every time they went to the clinic, she locked herself up in her room, then snuck out through the window and visited the clinic with Dominic."

"All so Rick wouldn't be traumatized," said Harriet. "And in the meantime Dominic managed to raise all kinds of suspicions about him being some kind of serial killer."

"He felt he did what he had to do for his family, consequences be damned," I said.

"Is she going to be all right?" asked Dooley. "Kristina, I mean?"

"It's too soon to tell," I said. "But so far things are looking good."

"I hope she'll be okay," said my friend. "And if not, she can always use Gran's money to buy herself an even better treatment."

"That money wasn't Gran's, Dooley," said Harriet, not for the first time. "She had to give it all back to the police the moment Omar was arrested."

"Too bad," said Dooley. "It could have bought Kristina a lot of cancer treatment."

"I think she'll be fine," I said. "Knowing that her daughter's killer is finally caught will go a long way to start healing that family."

"Do you think Omar's friends would have told the police?" asked Brutus.

"I don't know," I said. "Though judging from what Justina told us, I had the impression that Dunc, especially, was prepared to tell his fiancée the truth. Though I guess we'll never know for sure."

"I'm glad it all turned out all right," said Harriet. "And I'm also glad that we all worked together so well this time."

"Yeah, this was a team effort," I said. "And it took a team to bring Omar to justice."

Tex held up his arm, the signal Chase had been waiting for to come to his father-in-law's assistance, and he gladly left Scarlett and her Volvo brochures behind.

"I still think you should get a minivan," said Gran. "It's roomy, it's safe, and if you end up only having the one kid, you could take us all on holiday with you."

Chase's face revealed his abject horror at the prospect of taking Odelia's entire family on holiday with them. But then of course that's what you get: you don't just marry one person, you marry their whole family. For better or for worse. For richer, for poorer. In sickness and in health. And with a yellow Volvo station wagon or a roomy minivan.

THE END

Thanks for reading! If you want to know when a new Nic Saint book comes out, sign up for Nic's mailing list: nicsaint.com/news

EXCERPT FROM PURRFECT DOUBLE
(MAX 46)

Chapter One

The Karat Group's annual shareholders' meeting didn't exactly go as planned. The shareholders were all there, and so was the chairman of the board, Diedrich Karat, but the star of the show was of course current CEO Cotton Karat. Or at least he should have been, as he was expected to lead the meeting and discuss both the group's past year's financial results as well as future expected earnings and projections. Instead, all he seemed interested in was to salivate over his new girlfriend, the delectable Ebony Pilay.

Many a shareholder, from the lowliest ones, with only a few Karat Group shares in their investment portfolio, to the biggest specimens, proud to own a large chunk of the company, was stunned as the meeting progressed, and the group's current leader couldn't keep his eyes or his hands off his supermodel girlfriend. The fact alone that he'd placed her center stage for this all-important event was a blatant departure from tradition.

As far as the collected shareholders, and the denizens of

the financial press were aware, Ebony Pilay, though a well-known fashion model, owned no Karat Group shares, nor did she play any part in the group's organizational structure. She wasn't a CEO, CFO, COO or any of the other acronyms one often sees bandied about in the *Wall Street Journal*. Her only claim to that most coveted position next to the CEO was that she was his girlfriend. And Cotton Karat, the third scion of the Karat family to lead the luxury goods group, made sure no one could forget it. Lovey-dovey was one way to describe the scene.

It led to several members of the press corps to titter without inhibition, which was a strange spectacle to be sure. Usually the dreariest of journos, absolutely devoid of a sense of humor, and only perking up when being asked to write about interest rates or the price-to-earnings ratio, they now behaved as if they were all writing for the *National Enquirer*, ears red and eyes glittering with glee at this awful train wreck in progress.

Diedrich Karat, Cotton's dad and the group's previous CEO, looked as if he was barely hanging on to his equanimity. He'd already engaged in a bout of furious whisperings with the group's legal advisor Tobias Pushman, but what could they do? They couldn't berate Cotton in public, or frogmarch his girlfriend off the stage. The rest of the group's main players, all gathered on that stage, seemed to have accepted their role in the drama, and adopted a policy of grinning and bearing it and trying to act as if this was the most natural thing in the world, and not a complete meltdown of one of the country's biggest concerns.

The Karat Group's stock was trading at a thousand dollars a share at the start of the meeting. By the time the meeting finally adjourned, the stock had dropped to five hundred a share. One hundred billion dollars in value had been erased from the market cap. In other words: the single-largest drop in share price since the crash of 2001.

***

"Have you completely lost your mind?!"

"It's just a dip, Dad," Cotton said.

"A dip? A DIP?!"

Tobias Pushman, the group's legal beagle, gave his former boss and current chairman of the board a look of concern. Diedrich's face had turned the color of a ripe tomato. Drops of sweat were beading the man's brow and skipping down his temples, and his hair was matted to his sizable dome. If his blood pressure kept rising, a coronary was a given.

"Sir, I think you better sit down," Tobias suggested.

"I won't sit down until this matter is resolved and resolved to my satisfaction!" Diedrich thundered, swinging his arms dangerously. "Do you realize what you've done? You've singlehandedly wrecked the group! Reduced us to a Wall Street laughingstock!"

"You're exaggerating, Dad," said Cotton, who'd placed his sneakered feet up on his desk and was throwing a stress ball into the air with his left hand and deftly catching it with his right. "So the stock dropped a couple of points. It'll self-correct. You'll see."

"It won't self-correct," said Diedrich, shaking with right-eous anger at so much ignorance. "It will self-destruct if you keep fornicating with this… this… this Jezebel!"

"Hey, Ebony is a highly respected and extremely successful model, Dad. Twenty *Vogue* covers and counting. And we weren't fornicating. We were merely displaying our mutual affection."

"It's not done, son! You can't organize a petting session at the annual shareholders' meeting!"

"It's not a good look," Tobias agreed.

Diedrich threw a copy of the *Wall Street Journal* onto his son's desk. The headline screamed, 'Cotton Kills Karat.' "If you keep this up, we're toast, Cotton. Toast!"

"I'm sure it's not as bad as all that," Cotton tut-tutted.

"It's worse! They're predicting we'll be ripe for a hostile takeover bid before the end of the next fiscal quarter. Our shareholders are all threatening to sue!"

Cotton rolled his eyes. He didn't seem overly concerned. On his desk, a framed picture of Ebony Pilay held pride of place. It was the first of many *Vogue* covers she'd graced with her willowy presence, and she was staring into the lens as lusciously as she had gazed at Cotton at that fateful meeting.

"Just imagine if Warren Buffett brought a supermodel to Berkshire Hathaway's annual meeting," said Diedrich, "and instead of talking about the value of the company portfolio spent two hours canoodling with his girlfriend instead! The man would be vilified!"

"Now you're simply being dramatic," said Cotton as he aimed the ball at a mini basketball hoop in the corner of his office and hit it on the first try. "And now if you'll both excuse me, I've got a lunch date with Ebony, and the lady doesn't like to be kept waiting."

And watched on by his dumbfounded dad and his apoplectic legal advisor, the youngest CEO in the business left the room, carelessly humming *You're still the one.'*

***

For a moment, silence reigned in the room, then Diedrich turned a look of desperation to the man whose legal acumen was only rivaled by his unparalleled knack for designing daring schemes, and said, "Give me something, Tobias. Anything."

Tobias, a swarthy man with thick brows that concealed two cold blue eyes, steepled his fingers and brought them to his lips. "I think I might have an idea for you, sir."

"What is it?"

"It's a little risky, but it might offer a solution for all of our problems."

"Does it involve murdering Cotton and making it look like an accident?"

"Not exactly, sir. Though it does involve putting him on ice for a little while."

Diedrich allowed himself to drop down in one of the wingback chairs in the big office. His face was still an unhealthy shade of puce, and judging from the veins throbbing in his neck, the man was in urgent need of his blood pressure medication. "What did you have in mind?"

"Have you ever seen a French comedy named 'Le Con,' sir?"

"I'm not really into French comedy, though I have a feeling I'm in one right now. Though it could also be a French horror movie."

"In the movie, the CEO of one of those big French conglomerates finds himself at the center of some serious fracas, so his assistant comes up with the brilliant idea of replacing him with a double. The double is just a nobody, of course, with no real powers or authority. A puppet, if you will, controlled by the company's board of directors."

"A double?"

The sharpest legal mind ever to graduate from NYU nodded earnestly. "We ship Cotton off to the Heartfield Clinic, where he can be cured of his sex addiction. We buy off Miss Pilay so she will sever all ties with Cotton, and while your son is safely tucked away at Heartfield, a double takes his place, his every decision controlled by us."

"I see," said Diedrich thoughtfully. "And where do you propose we find this idiot?"

The lawyer's lips formed a devious moue. "Oh, I have one lined up for us already, sir."

Chapter Two

Eric Blandine was a man as bland as his name suggested. He was a lowly worker drone who'd spent his entire adult life stocking tins of foie gras, drums of caviar and boxes of exclusive pralines in one of the many warehouses that furnished these delicacies to airport stores and gift shops supplied by the Karat Group. And he was just fulfilling a large order of foie gras and boxing them up for imminent shipment when a low whistle sounded in his rear. He turned, and found himself looking at his buddy James Perkins.

"Boss wants to see you, Goldie," said Jimmy with a cheeky grin.

Due to Eric's uncanny resemblance to Cotton Karat, his colleagues had gotten into the habit of referring to him with the unoriginal nickname Goldie, short for karat gold.

"What does he want to see me for?" asked Eric, who didn't like to be disturbed when he was boxing up an order. He was one of those people who liked to do things the proper way, and being interrupted like this irked his sense of appropriate order and protocol.

"Your girlfriend probably dropped by," said Jimmy.

"Girlfriend?" asked Eric, carefully descending the metal ladder and balancing the half-filled box in the crook of his elbow.

"Ebony, of course. Though to be honest I don't know what she sees in you, Goldie."

"Must be all of his billions," said Margie, another one of

Eric's colleagues. She stood leaning against the rack, taking a break.

"Or his sex appeal," said Jimmy. "Let's not forget about Goldie's amazing sex appeal."

"Did you see him at that meeting the other day?" asked Margie.

"What meeting?" asked Eric, good-naturedly going along with the gentle ribbing. He was used to it by now, and didn't mind.

"That big shareholders' meeting. Goldie here kissing and fondling Ebony in front of a room full of stiffs. Looked like he was having a great old time, weren't you, Goldie?"

"Oh, absolutely," said Eric as he carefully placed down the box. "A wonderful time."

"I wonder what Maisie thinks about all this, though," said Jimmy, referring to Eric's wife.

"I'll bet she's fine with it," said Margie. "She's a forgiving wife, our Maisie is."

"She certainly is," said Eric with a smile.

"What do you think you're doing!" suddenly a voice rang out through the warehouse. "Get a move on, Blandine! The boss don't got all day, you know!"

"Yeah, hop to it, Goldie," Margie urged him on. "Let's not keep Ebony waiting."

"I'm coming!" Eric cried, and hurried off, watched on by his grinning colleagues.

He entered the office, fully expecting to find Norm there, eager to discuss the plans for his upcoming vacation, but instead he found Norm accompanied by two men he'd never seen before, though one of them looked slightly familiar for some reason.

"Eric, please take a seat," said Norm, and gestured to a chair in front of his desk.

"Yes, sir," said Eric meekly, and quickly sat down, nervously rubbing his hands on his blue jumpsuit as he did.

Much to his surprise, he found the older of the two visitors eyeing him closely. The man, who was probably in his early sixties, and had one of those big flabby faces, even brought his face so close to his that he could smell the cigar smoke emanating from him.

"Mh," said the man finally. "You were right, Tobias. It is uncanny."

"Isn't it?" said the other man. He was dressed in an expensive suit, was clean-shaven and had one of those square jaws that reminded Eric of a G-man. He also had heavy brows that half-obscured two sharp eyes that were coldly scrutinizing him. Like a fishmonger studying a halibut and deciding how best to slice and dice it for later consumption.

"Eric," said Norm, "these two gentlemen have a special request for you."

"Oh?" said Eric, wondering if they were here to place a large order of foie gras.

"Do you know who I am?" asked the older man.

"No, sir," said Eric truthfully.

"This is Diedrich Karat," said Norm.

Eric stared at the man. Then his eyes traveled to the large picture suspended on the wall behind Norm. It was the same man, only looking slightly younger and a lot skinnier. Eric's eyes went wide. "Mr. Karat?" he asked, his voice sounding squeaky to his own ears.

"That's right," said Mr. Karat, nodding with satisfaction at the other man's consternation.

"Has anyone ever told you that you are the spitting image of Mr. Karat's son Cotton, Eric?" asked the younger man, who hadn't yet been introduced.

Eric nodded wordlessly.

"His colleagues all call him Goldie," said Norm. "For karat

gold?" he added when the two men turned bland faces to him.

"Is that so?" said Mr. Karat with a sort of avuncular smile that didn't quite become him. Like a shark trying to affect a grin at its prey. "Well, I don't know if you're aware of this, Eric, but my son has recently found himself in a spot of trouble."

Once again Eric nodded wordlessly. He now realized he was clenching his buttocks to a painful extent, and that his armpits were twin pools of sweat. It's not every day that you suddenly find yourself in the presence of the big boss of your company.

"Cotton needs to go away for a couple of weeks, Eric," the G-man took over the narrative. "And in the meantime we would like you to replace him."

Eric's butt-clenching intensified. "You do?" he squeaked.

"Only for a couple of weeks, mind you," said Mr. Karat. "While Cotton works through a few issues that are of no concern to you."

"But..." Eric began, but was immediately silenced by a look of warning from Norm.

"You'd be doing the company a huge favor," said the G-man.

"It's important that no one find out about Cotton disappearing from the scene," Mr. Karat explained. "Our investors might get antsy. They're like vultures, you see. One sign of weakness and they're likely to attack and rip the flesh from our bones."

"And that's where you come in," said the G-man, towering over Eric, as was Mr. Karat. If they'd have aimed a spotlight at his face he wouldn't have been surprised. "We need you to make sure things at the Karat Group look as if it's all business as usual. Though of course we'll shield you off as much as we can. All you need to do is look the part."

"B-b-but…" sputtered Eric.

"*Look* the part but not *act* the part. I mean in meetings or negotiations with clients."

"We'll take care of all that," Mr. Karat assured him. "All you have to do is show up and make it look as if Cotton is right where he should be, in complete control of the company."

"We don't have to tell you that discretion is an absolute necessity," said the other man.

"You're not to breathe a word about this to anyone, you hear?" said Mr. Karat.

"Not to your wife, not to your friends or colleagues. Absolutely no one."

"And when all is said and done, you'll be handsomely rewarded."

Eric's ears pricked up. "Rewarded?" he squeaked.

"Handsomely."

He swallowed as he thought about this for a moment. "I'm not sure if…" he began.

"Eric, this is not a proposition," said Norm warningly. "This is an assignment."

"The most important assignment you'll ever get," said Mr. Karat.

"I don't know about this…" he muttered helplessly.

The two men converged on him, their combined bulk making him shrink and cower. "You want to help your employer, don't you, Eric?" said Mr. Karat. "Be a loyal company man?"

"Well, of course, but…"

"Stock options," said the G-man with a cold smile as his eyes bored into Eric's.

"Yes, we'll give you stock options," said Mr. Karat. "Stock options that will make you a very rich man indeed, Mr. Blandine. Stock options that will ensure a future for you and for your family. An unencumbered future for you and your loved ones. How does that sound?"

"Good," he admitted as he wondered if he'd ever be able to go to the bathroom again.

"This is not a negotiation, Blandine," said Norm, as he also got up from behind his desk and joined the browbeating exercise. "This is an order. You will pretend to be Cotton Karat from now on, and you will not mention this to anyone. Is that clear?!"

He meekly nodded. It was perfectly clear. The only problem was: how was he ever going to explain all this to Maisie?

***

"I don't get it," said Maisie as she used a cotton pad to remove the makeup from her face. "Why do you have to go on a training weekend?"

"Not a weekend," Eric patiently explained, seated on the bed. "It's a training month."

"I've never heard such nonsense in my entire life. Why does a warehouse worker have to go train for a month? What are they going to teach you? How to print labels?"

"It's because of my promotion, Maisie," said Eric. "I already explained this to you."

"And I'm telling you I don't believe a word you're telling me. So try again, and this time please don't insult me and tell me the truth for a change."

"It is the truth, sweetheart. Norm called me into his office today and said I'm being promoted. From now on I'm going to be team leader. And all team leaders have to train for a month in Garden City. It's standard company policy."

Maisie made a skeptical noise as she studied her face in the mirror. She was a large woman, with coarse features and a square doughy face. But even though she wasn't exactly pretty, she was the apple of Eric's eye, and had been since the day they met in high school. It wasn't so much that they'd fallen in love at first sight and had become high school sweethearts, but more that one day Maisie decided Eric would make a suitable husband and father to her kids and told him that from now on she was his girlfriend. And Eric, meek as usual, had simply accepted her dictum. Not that he had a lot of choice in the matter. When Maisie made a decision, that was the way it was, no back talk allowed.

She now fixed her husband with a curious look. "You're lying to me, Eric."

"No, I'm not," he said weakly.

"I can tell from the way your nose is twitching. It's your tell."

"My nose isn't twitching," he said quietly, as his hand surreptitiously traveled to the traitorous appendage and took a firm hold of his schnoz.

Maisie planted both hands on her hips, a clear sign she was fed up with this nonsense. "Enough of this, Blandine. You better start telling me the truth in one—two—three…"

"All right, all right!" he finally cried. "Mr. Karat and his lawyer were in the office today, and they told me I have to pretend to be Cotton Karat for a couple of weeks, while Cotton is off to some clinic somewhere to get cured of his sex addiction. They don't want anyone to find out about it since it might sink the stock price even further than it's already sunk and because I look so much like Cotton they chose me to be his double."

Whatever Maisie had expected, it clearly wasn't this. But the story was so unlikely, so outrageous, so crazy, that it simply had to be true. "Well, I'll be damned," she finally said.

"They're giving me stock options," Eric said, not meeting his wife's gaze. "A lot of stock options. And if I manage to pull this off, and make the stock go up again, I'll be a rich man. Or so they said."

"How much?" said Maisie curtly. She wasn't the kind of woman to hem and haw, but as usual went straight to the heart of the matter.

"Ten stock options at five hundred dollars a share. If the stock starts trading at last week's price again, they'll be worth ten thousand."

"And if they keep sinking, they'll be worth zilch." She thought for a moment. "What about Ebony Pilay?"

"She's out of the picture. They bought her off."

Maisie uttered an incredulous laugh. "Of course they did. And I'll bet they offered her a lot more than ten measly stock options."

Eric shrugged. "It wasn't a negotiation, sweetheart. It was either this or I wasn't going to have a job anymore. Plus they'd blackball me. Make sure I won't find a job elsewhere."

She thought for a moment, then finally nodded, her black eyes glittering. "You'll go through with this, and when you're halfway through the assignment you'll ask for another ten options." And when her husband started to protest she held up her hand. "Don't you see? They need you more than you need them. How many Cotton lookalikes do you think there are in this country? They must be desperate to hatch such a ridiculous scheme." She rubbed her hands. "This is our chance to make some serious moolah. Lots and lots of it."

Eric sighed and let himself drop down on the bed.

He had a feeling his troubles had only just begun.

Chapter Three

I was peacefully sleeping at the foot of Odelia's bed and dreaming of some prime kibble when suddenly a loud scream brutally tore through the gossamer cobweb of my dream. The scream seemed to come from somewhere close by, and when I opened my eyes and lifted my head, I saw that it was actually Odelia herself who was screaming!

Immediately I rose up and padded across the bed to find out what was going on. Was the baby she was carrying kicking up a fuss? Had Odelia had a nightmare and had it thrown her for a loop? When you live with a human you soon realize anything is possible.

But when I joined her, I saw that she was staring at something on her pillow in horror. It wasn't Chase, for he was now supporting himself on one elbow and staring at the same spot, his face also contorted in abject shock.

And then I saw it: a mouse, placed neatly on the edge of Odelia's pillow.

Dooley, who'd been resting alongside me, now also came trotting up. He was smiling, and when I glanced over to him, he gave me a wink!

"It's a mouse," said Chase dully. As a detective, that was some quick thinking on his part.

"I can see it's a mouse," said Odelia. "But what is it doing there?"

"It looks dead," said Chase, as he gave the critter a gentle nudge with his finger.

"I don't get it," said Odelia. "So it crawled up onto my pillow in the middle of the night and then died?"

Both she and Chase now looked in my direction, as if expecting an explanation from yours truly. I could see why, of course. I'm a cat, you see, and cats are well known for being in the habit of catching mice and depositing them wherever takes their fancy.

"I didn't put it there," I assured them. "In fact I've never seen this mouse before."

To be absolutely honest, I'm not one for all this mouse-catching business. I always say live and let live, and that goes for every living creature under the sun—even mice.

"I put that mouse on your pillow," suddenly Dooley piped up, and he even looked proud as he spoke these immortal words.

"Dooley!" Odelia cried. "What the hell!"

Dooley's smile faltered. "I thought you'd like it," he said in his defense.

"You thought I'd enjoy finding a dead mouse on my pillow?!"

"Well…" he said. "Most humans seem to like it."

"Oh, Dooley," Odelia sighed as she stared at the offending dead animal some more.

"Did Dooley put it there?" asked Chase.

"He did. He thought it was a good idea."

"Have you been watching the Discovery Channel again?" I asked my friend.

Dooley nodded, looking a little shamefaced now. "There was a documentary on last night. About how cats always bring their humans little presents. Like mice and birds and… and worms and such. And the humans in the documentary seemed to like it."

"I'll bet they did," I said, shaking my head.

Odelia regretted her harsh rebuke when she saw Dooley's discomfiture. So she patted my friend's head and said, "It's very sweet of you to bring me a present, Dooley, but you didn't have to do that." She eyed him more closely. "Tell me you didn't kill that mouse?"

"Of course not!" said Dooley, horrified at the idea. "It was dead when I found it."

"Good," said Odelia. Clearly she didn't like the idea of her sweet cats turning into a couple of nocturnal predators all of a sudden.

"Where did you find it?" I asked, curious.

"In the field behind the house," said Dooley.

"It died a natural death," Odelia assured her husband.

Chase grunted something under his breath. He didn't seem overly concerned whether the mouse had died from old age or from an attack by some ravenous stalker. "I'll get rid of it," he said, and picked the mouse up by its tail, then carried it off, presumably to dump it in the compost bin for later disposal and subsequent recycling.

"Don't you think we should return it where Dooley found it?" I asked. "That mouse has a mother and a father, and sisters and brothers, who are probably wondering where it went off to all of a sudden."

"Better put it in the field," Odelia instructed her husband. "Let nature take its course."

"It will attract other, bigger animals," Chase warned.

Odelia shrugged. "We could give it a proper burial," she suggested.

Chase grinned, still holding the mouse between thumb and index finger. "A proper burial for a mouse?"

"It's a living, breathing creature, Chase. It deserves our respect."

Chase inspected the dead mouse. I had the impression he wanted to point out it wasn't breathing or living anymore, but he wisely refrained from stating the obvious. Instead, he said, "I'll stick it in the fridge for now. We can bury it later on."

And since Odelia and Chase were up, they decided to get ready for their day. The sun had hoisted itself over the horizon and was casting its rays into the room. Rise and shine!

"I don't get it," I told Dooley while Odelia took a shower and Chase rummaged around in search of a suitable coffin for the mouse. "Why would you think it's a good idea to put a dead mouse on Odelia's pillow?"

"It's the baby," my friend explained, looking pained. "Once the baby is born, it's going to take up a big chunk of Odelia's time and attention. And then what about me?"

"She'll still have time for us," I said. "It's not as if she'll suddenly forget all about us."

"She won't forget about you," Dooley clarified. "Because you're her favorite."

"I'm not her favorite," I said with a laugh.

"Oh, yes, you are. You solve crimes and make her look good. You're her ace sleuth, Max."

"Okay, so what about Harriet and Brutus? They're not ace sleuths and Odelia loves them just as much as she loves us."

"She loves Harriet because she's pretty, and Brutus because he's big and strong. But me? I don't have any special qualities, Max. I'm not smart like you, I'm not pretty like Harriet, and I'm not big and strong like Brutus. I'm... superfluous."

I was taken aback, both from hearing Dooley use such a difficult word, and by the meaning behind it. "You're not superfluous, Dooley. You're... sweet and cuddly."

He gave me a skeptical look. "Please. Sweet and cuddly is not an admirable quality."

"It is! And you're very sweet and very cuddly, Dooley."

But he didn't seem convinced. "I need a USP, Max."

"You mean UPS, surely?"

"No, I need a unique selling proposition. You and Harriet and Brutus all have one, and I also need one, or the moment that baby is born, they'll simply chuck me out."

"Nobody is going to chuck you out, Dooley."

"They will, unless I make myself indispensable. Which is why I thought of that mouse."

"I very much doubt you'll make yourself indispensable by festooning Odelia's pillow with dead mice."

"Yeah, she didn't seem to like it all that much, did she?"

"No, she did not."

We both looked on as Odelia removed the cover from the pillow and dumped it into the laundry basket, then picked up the pillow, thought for a moment, and dumped that into the laundry basket, too. Then she removed the cover from the duvet and put that in the laundry, and finally ended up putting both her and Chase's duvets into the laundry, as well as the mattress cover, and if Chase hadn't entered the room and stopped her, I had the impression she would have stripped the mattress off the bed, too, for deep cleaning.

No, Dooley's new USP wasn't exactly a big hit with this expectant mother.

ABOUT NIC

Nic has a background in political science and before being struck by the writing bug worked odd jobs around the world (including but not limited to massage therapist in Mexico, gardener in Italy, restaurant manager in India, and Berlitz teacher in Belgium).

When he's not writing he enjoys curling up with a good (comic) book, watching British crime dramas, French comedies or Nancy Meyers movies, sampling pastry (apple cake!), pasta and chocolate (preferably the dark variety), twisting himself into a pretzel doing morning yoga, going for a run, and spoiling his big red tomcat Tommy.

He lives with his wife (and aforementioned cat) in a small village smack dab in the middle of absolutely nowhere and is probably writing his next 'Mysteries of Max' book right now.

www.nicsaint.com

A Purrfect Gnomeful

Purrfect Cover

Purrfect Patsy

Purrfect Son

Purrfect Fool

Purrfect Fitness

Purrfect Setup

Purrfect Sidekick

Purrfect Deceit

Purrfect Ruse

Purrfect Swing

Purrfect Cruise

Purrfect Harmony

Purrfect Sparkle

Purrfect Cure

Purrfect Cheat

Purrfect Catch

Purrfect Design

Purrfect Life

Purrfect Thief

Purrfect Crust

Purrfect Bachelor

Purrfect Double

The Mysteries of Max Box Sets

Box Set 1 (Books 1-3)

Box Set 2 (Books 4-6)

Box Set 3 (Books 7-9)

Box Set 4 (Books 10-12)

Box Set 5 (Books 13-15)

Box Set 6 (Books 16-18)

Box Set 7 (Books 19-21)

Box Set 8 (Books 22-24)

Box Set 9 (Books 25-27)

Box Set 10 (Books 28-30)

Box Set 11 (Books 31-33)

Box Set 12 (Books 34-36)

Box Set 13 (Books 37-39)

Box Set 14 (Books 40-42)

The Mysteries of Max Big Box Sets

Big Box Set 1 (Books 1-10)

Big Box Set 2 (Books 11-20)

The Mysteries of Max Shorts

Purrfect Santa (3 shorts in one)

Purrfectly Flealess

Purrfect Wedding

Nora Steel

Murder Retreat

The Kellys

Murder Motel

Death in Suburbia

Emily Stone

Murder at the Art Class

Washington & Jefferson

First Shot

Alice Whitehouse

Spooky Times

Spooky Trills

Spooky End

Spooky Spells

Ghosts of London

Between a Ghost and a Spooky Place

Public Ghost Number One

Ghost Save the Queen

Box Set 1 (Books 1-3)

A Tale of Two Harrys

Ghost of Girlband Past

Ghostlier Things

Charleneland

Deadly Ride

Final Ride

Neighborhood Witch Committee

Witchy Start

Witchy Worries

Witchy Wishes

Saffron Diffley

Crime and Retribution

Vice and Verdict

Felonies and Penalties (Saffron Diffley Short 1)

The B-Team

Once Upon a Spy

Tate-à-Tate

Enemy of the Tates

Ghosts vs. Spies

The Ghost Who Came in from the Cold

Witchy Fingers

Witchy Trouble

Witchy Hexations

Witchy Possessions

Witchy Riches

Box Set 1 (Books 1-4)

The Mysteries of Bell & Whitehouse

One Spoonful of Trouble

Two Scoops of Murder

Three Shots of Disaster

Box Set 1 (Books 1-3)

A Twist of Wraith

A Touch of Ghost

A Clash of Spooks

Box Set 2 (Books 4-6)

The Stuffing of Nightmares

A Breath of Dead Air

An Act of Hodd

Box Set 3 (Books 7-9)

A Game of Dons

Standalone Novels

When in Bruges

The Whiskered Spy

ThrillFix

Homejacking

The Eighth Billionaire

The Wrong Woman

Printed in Great Britain
by Amazon